The Riley Bennett Series

The Terror of Two Cities

Andy Coltart

Published by New Generation Publishing in 2020

First Edition

Paperback ISBN: 978-1-80031-823-6
Ebook ISBN: 978-1-80031-822-9

www.newgeneration-publishing.com

New Generation Publishing

To my son, Sam

Acknowledgements

Firstly, to my friends Sally Carr and John Winterton, for helping with the editing of this book.

Secondly, to Russian model Kristina Maurer (@kris_maurer_official) and her photographer, Alex Dorofeev (@alexsecretph) for providing the amazing photo of her for the front cover.

Finally, to my friend Lizzy Biggs (@lizzybiggsphotography) for designing the covers.

Contents

Chapter 1

And So It Begins

The last month had been totally amazing. In fact, it had been life-changing. Riley had been struck by lightning during a hockey game at school several weeks ago. At the same time, her friends Casey and Alex were also hit. They'd not known each other before this incredible event. But after everything that followed since they had become close friends.

It was 7.30 a.m. and Riley sat in her room drying her hair. She could hear her brother and sister arguing over the toothpaste in the bathroom. This was an almost daily occurrence and one Riley had learnt to block from her mind. Instead she was thinking about the day ahead. Another day in Samson County High School. Something she used to dread, but thanks to her new friends and her special powers she was feeling much happier about going in.

You see, when the lightning struck Riley, Casey and Alex it created an electrical energy field that made them invisible to the rest of the world, but not to each other. Although this energy had faded in Casey and Alex it was still strong in Riley, possibly due to her epilepsy. Riley had learnt how to control her invisibility by matching the speed at which the electrical energy moved around her brain. She was now able to spin herself invisible and spin back again whenever she needed to.

Riley switched off her hairdryer and turned around in her chair. Lying on the bed were two outfits she'd picked for school. She decided to wear the crop top she and Casey had purchased recently at the mall. Once dressed, she made her way downstairs to find her mum busy making breakfast in the kitchen.

An hour earlier, Alex was out on his bike delivering papers. Although 6.30 a.m. is not most teenagers' idea of a good time to start the day, Alex was pleased to be up and delivering papers. His eyes had been affected by the lightning strike and although they weren't 100% better, they'd improved enough for him to use his bike again. Daylight was now taking over control of the sky, pushing away the night-time darkness. This made cycling easier as Alex headed home for some breakfast.

Casey lay in bed staring at her Presidential Medal of Freedom and her Secret Service I.D. *Who'd have thought this would be my life,* she thought to herself. Only a month ago she would have described herself as a rebel. But then the lightning struck and she met Riley and Alex. The friendship they now had was the best thing Casey had ever known. They had been through so much together. They'd saved the lives of kids in her school when the roof on the hall collapsed and they'd saved the American President when they foiled an assassination attempt. All in just a couple of weeks.

'You'd better be getting up,' shouted Mrs Johnson.

'I am,' replied Casey as she put her medal and I.D. back in her bedside table.

Around 7.45 a.m. she appeared in the kitchen in ripped jeans and a Nirvana T-shirt.

'Are you really wearing that to school?' asked her mum, knowing full well the answered would be yes.

'Yeah I am,' said Casey, sitting down and grabbing the cereal box on the table.

'Am I still dropping you at Casey's this morning?' said Mrs Bennett to Riley.

'Yes, please, Mom. We've decided to ride the bus together. Safety in numbers and all that,' said Riley.

'I'm glad you can do that as it takes the pressure off me trying to get the twins to school,' replied her mum.

'No problem, Mom. I'm just glad I don't have to ride the bus alone anymore. It was never a pleasant experience,' she replied.

AND SO IT BEGINS

Alex was on his way to college now. This was the first time he'd ridden his bike there in weeks. It felt so good to have that freedom again. His sight had been badly affected by the lightning strike but as the electrical energy in his brain dropped back to normal his sight had slowly recovered. Being virtually blind for a couple of weeks had made him more aware of others with that disability. He certainly valued the sight he now had so much more than he ever had in the past.

The doorbell rang, 'I'll get it, Mom,' said Casey. As she opened it, she saw Riley standing there. Mrs Bennett waved from the car before pulling away.

'Hey you, come on in,' said Casey.

'Nice T-shirt,' replied Riley.

'Yeah, try telling my mom that,' said Casey raising her eyebrows.

'You ready?' asked Riley.

'Yeah, just about,' said Casey, shoving a few books into her bag. Just as she finished there was a loud honk of a horn outside.

'The bus is here, you two,' shouted Casey's mum from upstairs.

'Okay Mom, see you later,' said Casey as she and Riley walked out of the house to board the bus.

Alex was locking his bike up in the racks at college when his friend Will came over.

'Hi there, bud, how you doing?' said Will.

'Great, thanks,' replied Alex, 'I finally got to ride my bike again.'

'So I see. How was it?' asked Will.

'Fine,' said Alex. The two of them went into the college and made their way to the cafe to grab their usual morning coffee before lectures began.

Much to Riley's amazement, no-one made a derogatory comment to her as she walked down aisle of the school bus.

Perhaps it was because Casey was with her, or maybe because she was now a national hero, having saved the life of the President. Either way she was grateful for a lapse in the usual bullying.

'Hi Riley, I haven't seen you for a few weeks,' said Josh, the baseball player from her school.

'Oh, hi Josh,' said Riley, smiling, 'no, I've had a few things going on.'

'So I've heard,' said Josh. 'How are you?'

'I'm good, thanks,' replied Riley. 'Oh, this is my friend Casey,' she added.

Josh, Riley and Casey sat together and talked at the back of the bus on the way to school. The girls told him as much as they could about their experience in the White House.

'Well, you two are definitely heroes,' he said, as the bus stopped outside the school and kids started to get off.

'See you later,' said Riley as she and Casey got off the bus and headed into school.

The main corridor was the usual frenzy of activity with students pushing past each other in a desperate attempt to reach their lockers before the bell rang.

'This place never changes, does it?' said Riley.

'No, it's always chaos first thing. I wonder if every school is like this in the morning?' replied Casey.

Just as they finished at their lockers, the bell rang loudly above them. It made Riley jump.

'You okay?' asked Casey.

'Yeah, just a little on edge as it's my first time on the hockey field this morning since the lightning strike,' said Riley.

'Don't worry, it'll be fine. I'll be there too. Let's see if we can get on the same team this time,' said Casey, as she headed off towards her classroom.

Once registration was over, Riley made her way to the changing rooms. Casey was waiting outside for her.

'You ready for this?' asked Casey.

'I guess so,' said Riley, as she pushed the door open.

The usual sight greeted their eyes. Clothes and hockey

sticks were scattered in a haphazard way across the floor. This made walking in a straight line near on impossible. Some of the girls were changed and ready, others were in various stages of undress. The muscular games teacher burst out of her room to shout at some girls who were more focussed on the mirror in the corner of the changing room than they were on getting ready.

'Two minutes, ladies,' she yelled before disappearing back into her room.

'We'd better be quick,' said Casey taking her Nirvana T-shirt off.

Having finished their coffees, Alex and Will made their way to the lecture theatre and took their seats. They'd got a visiting speaker today.

'I hope this guy is better than the last one they got in,' said Will.

'Me too, it'll be interesting to see if he can make ancient rock formations sound exciting,' said Alex, laughing.

Finally, everyone was changed and ready. The sports teacher led them out to the field.

'Are you two gonna be okay with this?' she asked Riley and Casey.

'We are, Miss, but could we be on the same team?' replied Casey.

'I'm sure I can arrange that,' said the teacher. Riley smiled, relieved she wasn't going to be stuck at the end of the field on her own this time. As they reached the field the teacher split the class into two groups, keeping her word and putting Riley and Casey together.

'Okay, girls, take your positions,' she said. One of the girls on Riley's team offered to go in goal this time. Riley volunteered to play up front.

'Wow, I never imagined you to be a forward,' said Casey.

'Well, I seem to have found a new confidence in myself after the last few weeks,' replied Riley.

The teacher blew into her whistle, sending its deafening screech across the field. The game got under way. The girls ran all over the field chasing the ball. Finally, it came to Riley and she set her eyes on the opposition's goal. She charged down the field, hitting the ball as she went. Others tried to stop her but she swerved past them all. At last she was clear. She jammed her foot into the mud to slow herself down. Then with an almighty swing of her hockey stick she launched the ball into the air. It flew like a rocket, past the goalie, before crashing into the back of the net. Her team could be heard cheering behind her.

'Nice one, Crazy Curls,' shouted one of the girls. The others looked at her with disapproval. 'Sorry, I meant Riley,' said the girl, realising what she'd said.

Leaving the lecture with other students, Will and Alex were commenting to each other how well the speaker had done.

'I have to admit he's the first one to leave me wanting to know more about the subject,' said Alex.

'Yeah, he was good,' said Will as they headed towards the library.

At the end of the game the girls were coated in mud. Riley and Casey's team didn't mind as they'd won the match. Riley had scored her first ever goal, partly due to the fact she'd not been stuck in goal for the first time in her school career.

'Right, you lot, showers!' bellowed the teacher as the girls entered the changing rooms.

The afternoon lessons seemed to fly by. Riley was watching the clock as she was looking forward to seeing their friend Alex at the end of the day. The final bell rang out and she wasted no time getting to her locker before the corridor was packed out with students.

'There you are,' said Riley to Casey as she finally appeared at her locker.

'Hi, yeah, sorry I'm late. My English teacher wants me to write an article for the school magazine about our role in stopping the assassination of the President,' said Casey.

'Wow, that's cool,' said Riley.

'Yeah it is, but I could do without the extra work on top of the homework he's handed out today,' replied Casey.

'Well, perhaps Alex and I can help you write it,' said Riley.

'That would be great,' replied Casey.

As the girls left the school building and walked down the steps, they could see Alex waiting on the sidewalk.

'Hey, you two,' he said, as they reached the bottom step. Riley didn't reply, she just gave him a hug and stepped aside so Casey could do the same.

'You ready for a drink?' asked Alex.

'Definitely,' replied Casey. The three of them headed off towards their favourite cafe near the library.

Chapter 2

Activation

'Coffees?' said Alex in an enquiring tone as they entered the cafe.

'Actually, I'm in the mood for a milkshake,' replied Riley.

'Me too,' added Casey.

'Okay,' said Alex, 'I'm guessing strawberry for both of you.'

'Well, of course,' said Riley, smiling and patting his shoulder as they left him at the counter and went to grab a seat on the sofa. A few minutes later Alex appeared with a tray of drinks and some chocolate cookies.

'Hey, what are these for?' said Casey.

'You looked like you needed one,' said Alex.

'Thanks,' said Riley.

'How did you know?' said Casey, smiling and collapsing back in on the sofa with a cookie in hand.

Meanwhile, in Washington DC the phone began to ring on Steve's desk. Picking it up, he said, 'National Security Advisor.'

The aide on the other end responded with, 'POTUS wants to see you immediately, sir.'

Straight away Steve put the phone down and got up from his desk, making his way through the West Wing of the White House to the Oval Office.

'You wanted to see me, Mr President,' he said, as he entered the room.

'Yes, Steve, come in,' said the President. 'Do you have an update on the attempted assassination investigation?' asked the President.

'Yes, sir, I do. As you're aware, the gun was brought into the White House via the linen delivery and placed in the

Blue Room by a cleaner named Jonny.'

'I am,' said the President.

'Well,' said Steve, 'this would not have been possible without Secret Service help, or their failure to follow procedure. To that end, we have had to begin an investigation into several agents on duty that morning.'

'And what have you discovered?' asked the President.

'It would appear one agent made the decision not to search the linen crates that morning,' said Steve. 'He has been suspended while further investigation takes place to establish whether he was in on the plot to kill you or just made a lapse in judgement in not doing his job properly that morning. Either way, he will no longer be on any White House detail in the future.'

'Very well,' said the President, 'keep me updated. Now we need to discuss Riley and her team.'

'Agreed, sir,' replied the National Security Advisor.

'So how was your day, Alex?' asked Riley.

'Not too bad actually,' replied Alex, 'we had an interesting speaker in a lecture today, which helped make the subject more interesting than normal.'

'What was the subject?' asked Casey.

'What ancient rock formations tell us about life on the planet,' said Alex.

'I wish I'd never asked!' said Casey, laughing.

'Look, I'm as keen as you to have Riley and her friends as part of the Secret Service. We rushed through making them agents,' said the President, 'but we need to do this right. Jack is the Director of Secret Service so he needs to be in on this. Also, their role will be wider than most agents and cross into other departments.'

'I agree, sir,' said Steve, 'we need the Director of the CIA, FBI and NSA involved too.'

'Can you set up a meeting?' asked the President.

'Yes, sir, I'll get it done,' said Steve.

Riley sat eating her cookie and watching her friends talking. Not many of us would be thankful for a lightning strike directly on us, but she was. The result had been two great friends and a chance to make a difference in the world.

'Hey dreamer, you with us?' said Casey to Riley.

'Err, yeah I'm here,' she replied, 'just thinking over everything that's happened to the three of us, that's all.'

'Well, we'd love you to join us in the present conversation,' said Casey.

'Yeah, sure, what are we talking about?'

'Christine,' said Alex.

'What about her?' asked Riley.

'Just wondering if you'd spoken to her much in the last couple of weeks since her dad was reported to the police,' said Alex.

'Yeah a couple of times,' replied Riley.

'And?' said Casey.

'And what?' said Riley.

'And how is she, and what's the latest news?' said Alex.

'Oh, yeah, she's okay. Things have calmed down at home and she and her mom are getting on well. Her dad has been charged with assault. He'll be in court soon.'

'It's all so sad,' said Casey.

'It is,' said Alex, 'but it's better this way than Christine suffering in silence.'

'That's true,' said Casey.

'I'm almost afraid to ask,' said Alex, 'but what's happened to the three mean girls who assaulted you, Riley?'

'Oh yeah, I meant to tell you both. They've agreed to be moved to a school for kids with behavioural problems instead of going to court and being charged with assault. It seemed like a win/win as they're not at our school now but they get one more chance to get things right before getting a criminal record,' said Riley.

'They got off too lightly, in my view,' said Casey.

'Possibly,' said Riley, 'but remember, we changed our minds about Christine's bullying when we learnt her story. I like the idea of giving people second chances and not just judging them.'

'Sounds like a good set of values to have,' said Alex.

'I think so,' said Riley.

Suddenly all of their phones started to beep simultaneously. Taking them out they each read the same message. 'United States Secret Service team activation - report to CIA H.Q., Langley immediately!' Casey dropped the cookie she was eating.

'Oh my God!' she said, rather louder than she intended. Riley and Alex looked at each other.

'Wow,' said Alex, 'it's really happening!'

'Looks like it,' said Riley, placing her milkshake back on the table.

'So, what do we do now?' said Casey.

'I text back,' said Riley, 'and ask for more details.'

'Good idea,' said Casey.

Riley responded to the message on behalf of the three of them. She asked for some details and was told the following: their schools and parents had been informed during the day that the three of them would be going to Washington for three months to work in schools on the White House Youth Ambassadors' Programme. They knew this was a Secret Service cover for their true role. They were told that plane tickets had been sent to their homes and that they would be met by the Secret Service at Ronald Reagan National Airport in Washington DC tomorrow afternoon.

'It looks like we will have to wait until we're in DC to find out the rest of what's going to happen,' said Riley.

'Three months!' said Casey. 'My mom won't be happy with me missing that much school!'

'Perhaps that issue has been addressed in the information parents have received,' said Alex.

'I hope so,' said Casey.

'I guess we'd all better head home,' said Riley.

'Let's talk online later,' said Alex. The girls agreed and they all got up and left their favourite cafe wondering when they'd see it again.

The President was on his phone in the Oval Office.

'So, this is in the diary for tomorrow, then?' he asked.

'Yes, sir,' replied Steve, 'we'll meet with the Directors of the CIA, NSA, FBI and the Secret Service at 11.00 a.m. Then at 2.00 p.m. we can introduce them to Riley, Casey and Alex. After that, Jack, from the Secret Service, will take the three of them for a briefing with himself and James, the CIA agent who dealt with their recruitment process.'

'Very good,' replied the President.

As Riley turned the key in the front door, it was pulled open before she could push it herself.

'Hi Riley,' yelled Beth and Max, her sister and brother.

'Let her through the door,' said their mum, pulling the twins back so Riley could get inside.

'How was your day?' asked Mrs Bennett.

'Okay,' replied Riley, 'I scored my first ever goal in hockey today.'

'Oh well done,' replied her mum.

'Mom,' said Riley, 'we need to talk.'

'Yes, we do,' replied Mrs Bennett, holding up a letter with the President's seal at the top of it. 'Beth, Max, go and get changed into your pyjamas and then you can watch some television,' said their mum.

Riley walked through to the kitchen and put the kettle on.

'So, what does the letter say?' she asked her mum.

'Well, it says the President wants you in Washington for three months. Apparently, the White House has arranged for you to have your lessons in DC while you take part in the Youth Ambassadors' Programme.'

'So, can I go then?'

'I'm not sure,' replied Mrs Bennett, 'three months is an awfully long time.'

'I know, but it's the President asking. Plus, we knew this would be asked of us after what we did to save him,' said Riley.

'True,' said Mrs Bennett.

'So, can I go?'

'I guess so. But I want you to keep in touch every day,' said her mum.

'I will,' said Riley, jumping up and down on the spot with excitement. She went over to her mum and gave her an enormous hug.

'Hey, what's going on?' said Beth coming into the kitchen.

'I'm going to Washington to work for the President,' said Riley.

'That's not fair,' said Beth, 'why can't I work for the President?'

'Perhaps you will when you're older,' said her mum.

Alex was sitting at the kitchen table holding the White House letter when his father came in from work.

'Hi son, how was your day,' said Mr Manning. 'What's that you're holding?'

'It's a letter for you from the President,' said Alex.

'Oh,' said his father, 'pass it here, then. I'd better take a look.'

Alex made some coffee while his father read the letter. Sitting down together at the table in the kitchen, his father asked, 'So, what do you know about this?'

'Only what I was told in a text,' said Alex.

'And what was that?' asked his father.

'That the President wants Riley, Casey and me in Washington for three months to take part in this Youth Ambassadors' Programme and that we will continue to get our education in DC while we do it.'

'Well, son, what do you think? Is it something you want to do?' asked Mr Manning.

'Absolutely,' replied Alex, 'this is a huge opportunity and one I'd be mad to miss out on.'

'I have to agree, son,' said his father, 'as much as I'll miss you not being here, I think this is too important an opportunity to miss.'

'So, I can go then?' asked Alex.

'Of course, son,' replied his father. 'You'll have to keep me updated with what you get up to, though,' he added. Alex just smiled, knowing full well that a lot of what he would be doing would be classified.

Casey and her parents were sitting round the dinner table eating the meatloaf her mum had made that morning.

'This is great, love,' said her dad to her mum. 'Just what I need before another night shift.'

Casey looked at them both, wondering who would bring up the letter first. Neither seemed to be doing so. She was on tenterhooks wondering if she could go and couldn't wait any longer. So, bursting from her mouth like a dam breaching came the words,

'So, Washington, the President, ambassadors, me, can I go?'

'Do you want to say that again, sweetheart, perhaps in a sentence that makes sense?' said her dad.

Casey composed herself and tried again. 'So, can I go to DC tomorrow to work for the President?' she asked. Her parents looked confused.

'What are you talking about?' asked her mum.

'I was told you'd had a letter from the White House,' said Casey.

'I don't think so,' said her mum, 'just the usual junk I've put in the trash.'

Casey jumped up from the table and took the lid off the bin, pulling out various flyers for pizza places and the local newspaper.

'What are you hoping to find?' asked her dad.

'This!' said Casey handing him an envelope with the Seal of the President of the United States on the back.

'Oh my,' said her mum, 'can't believe I binned that!'

'I can,' said Mr Johnson, laughing.

Mr Johnson opened the letter and read it before passing it to his wife.

'So, do you want to go?' he asked Casey.

'Definitely,' she replied.

'Just hold fire one second,' said Mrs Johnson, 'this isn't a weekend away, it's three months.'

'I know, Mom, but they've sorted school for us,' said Casey.

'It is a great opportunity,' her dad interjected, supporting her.

'You're right,' said Mrs Johnson, 'it just seems a long time to be away.'

'Mom, I'll call you every day,' added Casey.

Finally, her mum gave in and agreed she could take part. That evening Riley, Casey and Alex were all busy packing for the journey the following morning. They all received another text from the Secret Service with a kit list. Riley had decided to add her sketchbook and a teddy to that list.

Chapter 3

The Flight to DC

Riley put on her pyjamas and went downstairs to make a hot chocolate.

'Are you all packed and ready?' asked her mum.

'I think so,' replied Riley. 'Mom, I'm gonna go to my room and call Alex and Casey,' she added.

'Okay, but don't be up too late, you have a busy day ahead of you tomorrow,' replied her mum.

Riley promised to get to bed by 10.30 p.m. and gave her mum a hug before going back to her room with her drink.

'Hey guys,' said Riley, as she sat in her bedroom at her computer.

'Hi,' replied Casey and Alex.

'So how did your evenings go with your parents?' asked Riley.

Alex went first, saying how supportive his father had been and what a relief it was to not have to argue with him.

'He negotiates million-dollar deals so there's no way to win an argument with him,' said Alex.

Casey explained how her mum had binned the President's letter so knew nothing about it.

'Oh my God!' said Riley.

'It's okay,' said Casey. 'I found it and my dad was great at helping persuade my mum I should go.'

'So, does that mean we are all packed and ready to go?' asked Alex.

The girls both replied: 'Yes.'

'That's great,' said Alex, 'I'm so looking forward to going back to Washington.'

'I have a feeling this trip is going to be a lot of hard work,' said Riley.

'Yeah, but it will be so worth it,' said Alex.

The three of them talked for a while longer about being

away from home for so long and what they thought they'd really be doing in DC.

Eventually Riley said, yawning, 'I'm gonna go to bed, guys; I'll see you at the airport at 9.00 a.m.'

The others both said goodnight and went offline. Riley walked across the rug on her floor, her bare feet sinking into its fluff, and climbed into bed. Pulling the covers up around her, she switched off the light and lay there in the dark. She was thinking about the trip and particularly what would be asked of her with her unique powers. Eventually she fell asleep.

In what seemed like no time at all, the 'beep, beep, beep' of Riley's alarm woke her up. There was no sunshine coming through the gap in her curtains this morning. Riley got out of bed and went to the window to look out. A dull grey sky greeted her. *At least it's not raining,* she thought to herself as she grabbed her towel and headed for the bathroom.

'Hey, you two, out you go!' she said to Beth and Max.

As her brother and sister filed out of the room Riley locked the door behind them. Taking off her pyjamas she noticed the scar on her thigh from the lightning strike. She stepped into the shower and was glad to feel the warmth of the water on her skin, as the bathroom had felt colder than usual.

'Are you going to be long in there?' said Casey's mum, banging on their bathroom door.

'No, Mom,' came the reply. Casey was wrapping her wet hair in a towel, having just finished in the shower.

'Good,' said her mum, 'breakfast is nearly ready.'

Alex was showered, dressed and sitting drinking coffee with his father around the same time the girls were both occupying their respective bathrooms.

'You sure this is what you want to do?' asked Mr Manning.

'Yeah, Dad, I'm sure,' replied Alex.

'Okay then, I'll take you to the airport in an hour,' said his father.

'Thanks, Dad,' replied Alex.

Alex was feeling much more confident in the last week or so as a result of the steady improvement in his sight.

Riley appeared a short time later, having finished in the bathroom and got herself dressed.

'You hungry?' asked her mum.

'Not very,' replied Riley.

'Probably nerves,' said her mum.

If only she knew! Riley's stomach was turning somersaults. Her mind was all over the place thinking about meeting the Secret Service, training with them, possible missions and so on. She wondered if she'd ever feel relaxed enough to eat breakfast ever again!

'Well, you should probably try and have something,' her mum continued, placing a bowl of cereal in front of her.

'We'd better get going,' said Casey's mum, finishing the coffee she was holding.

Casey got up from the table and cleared her plate away. She then grabbed her bags from the bottom of the stairs and waited for her mum to open the door.

'Do you need a hand with anything?' asked Mrs Johnson.

'I'm fine,' said Casey, as they left the house and went to put everything in the car.

'Sorry your dad wasn't here to see you off,' said her mum.

'It's okay,' said Casey, 'we said goodbye last night before he left for work.'

A short time later Riley, Casey and Alex were all standing together at the airport.

'Please tell me you both have your passports and Secret Service I.D.,' said Alex.

'Of course, we do,' replied Riley.

'Just checking,' said Alex.

'Okay, you three,' said Mr Manning, 'that's your bags checked in and your boarding cards sorted. You can go through to departures when you're ready.'

They each took a moment to say goodbye to their parents. Riley's mum was getting a bit tearful so Riley decided it was time to go before she lost it altogether and embarrassed them all.

The three of them set off towards the security checkpoint and passed their hand luggage over for scanning. Stepping through the gate, they were now in the departure lounge.

'Let's get a coffee while we wait for our flight,' said Alex.

'Good idea,' said Casey. They found a cafe with seats that looked out over the runway. They could see planes taking off and landing.

'That'll be us soon enough,' said Riley.

'At least we're on a plane this time instead of a long train ride,' said Casey.

The last time they'd travelled to Washington together was when they'd prevented the assassination of the President. They'd taken an overnight train to get there.

Suddenly an announcement for their flight to Ronald Reagan National came across the tannoy.

'Guess we'd better head to the gate,' said Alex.

The three of them got up and followed the signs to gate eleven where their plane was waiting.

'Good morning,' said the flight attendant at the desk.

'Can I have your tickets and I.D. please,' asked the attendant. They all handed their tickets over and took out their Secret Service I.D.

'Oh,' said the attendant, looking at their badges, 'have a safe flight, Special Agents.'

'Thank you,' said Alex as they walked onto the ramp leading to the plane.

Once on board they found their seats in business class.

'Wow, I had no idea we were in these seats!' said Casey.

'Didn't you read your ticket?' asked Riley.

'Clearly not,' said Alex before Casey could answer.

They made themselves comfortable and a stewardess came around and offered them a drink before take-off.

Once they were in the air, they were able to take their seatbelts off and move around. Alex had been in the row in front of the two girls so he got up and stood in the aisle to talk to them. They'd only been talking for ten minutes or so when a stewardess from economy class came through to speak to them.

'Excuse me, but are you Secret Service?' she asked.

'Why do you ask?' replied Riley.

'We have a situation we need help with,' she replied.

'What is it?' asked Alex.

'There's a man threatening to hurt other passengers,' she said. 'He's out of his seat and very angry.'

Riley, Casey and Alex looked at each other. They were all thinking the same thing – *we're not trained for this!*

Alex walked to the curtain that separated economy from business class to take a look.

'Leave this with us,' he said to the stewardess.

The girls looked at him, slightly shocked that he'd made the decision for the team without talking to them.

'Look, we can handle this,' he said. 'Riley, can you make yourself invisible and get behind him?'

'I can try,' she said.

'Casey, you and I will confront him and Riley will jump on him from behind. Once he's down we can restrain him until the flight lands.'

The girls agreed and Riley went to the bathroom to spin invisible.

Ever since she was struck by lightning Riley had had some electrical energy spinning round her brain. It had stayed there because of her epilepsy. She had discovered that if she spun her body at the same speed the energy field would widen, making her invisible to everyone except Alex and Casey, who had also been struck by the same lightning bolt. It was tight in the aeroplane bathroom, even more so than a cubicle at school, but Riley managed to spin and bring on a burning feeling in her brain. This told her she was invisible, so she made her way back to the others.

Casey looked at Riley's hand: the skin was shimmering.

'Yup, she's invisible,' she said to Alex.

'Okay, let's go,' said Alex.

He sounded so confident and full of authority. Riley and Casey followed him. When they reached the man, he was standing in the middle of the aisle. He looked up from the passenger he was yelling at.

'What do you two kids want?' he said. Alex showed him his badge.

'Sir, I'm US Secret Service, I'd like you to take your seat please,' said Alex.

The man looked at Alex and then Casey. Laughing he said, 'Yeah right, you and whose army?'

While he was talking, Riley had got on her tummy on the floor and was crawling past the three of them in the only space she could find. Moments later she was up on her feet behind the man.

'Oh, I don't need an army,' said Alex as he nodded to Riley.

Riley had put some distance between herself and the man and was now running at him. She jumped, flinging her arms round his head and neck, and her legs round his waist. The unexpected force from behind made him topple forward. He crashed onto the floor in the aisle like a sack of potatoes.

Casey and Alex had stepped back to make way for this spectacular take down. They now stepped in and grabbed the man's arms, pulling them behind his back as Riley climbed off him.

'Have you got some rope or cord?' he asked the stewardess.

'Sorry, no we don't,' she replied.

'Here,' said one of the women in a seat nearby, as she pulled the cord from her child's dressing gown.

'Thanks,' said Alex as he tied the man's hands behind his back.

They took the man through to business class as there

were seats available and fewer passengers.

'Sit there,' said Alex, 'and keep quiet.'

The man sat down still dazed from his take down. Riley went to the bathroom and came back visible again. Casey asked the stewardess to contact the ground and request agents board the plane to remove the man before other passengers disembarked, which she did.

When the plane came into land at Ronald Reagan National Airport, police cars could be seen heading towards it on the tarmac, their lights flashing and sirens sounding. Once the doors were opened, security and police boarded the plane. The Secret Service agent sent to meet Riley and friends also came aboard.

'I'm Agent Jacobs; I hear you three have started work early today!' he said.

'Yeah, sorry about that,' said Riley.

'Oh, don't be sorry, you've done a good job keeping the passengers safe on this flight,' replied Agent Jacobs.

Riley smiled; this was why she'd agreed to do this, so she could help people. The agent talked to the police and then turned to Riley, Casey and Alex.

'We are okay to leave for the White House as long as you all provide the police with a statement by the end of the day,' he said.

'That's fine with us,' said Alex.

The three of them followed Agent Jacobs through the airport, collecting the bags on the way. He had a black 4x4 waiting for them outside. It had blacked-out windows and looked like it was a White House vehicle. Riley got into the front and Casey and Alex sat in the back as they left the airport and headed across the Potomac River into Washington DC.

Chapter 4

Security Meeting

A short time later they were pulling into the White House grounds.

'Leave your bags in the car for now,' said Agent Jacobs, who'd driven them. They all got out and went inside.

'Hello again,' said Steve, the National Security Advisor, 'welcome back to the White House. If you'd like to follow me the President's Chief of Staff is waiting for you.'

They followed Steve to a large room with chairs set around a long rectangular table.

'Take a seat, guys,' said the National Security Advisor, 'Grace will be with you shortly.'

Sure enough, they were only there for a minute before the door opened and in walked the President's Chief of Staff.

'Good afternoon everyone, my name is Grace and I'm here to brief you before the President meets with you. Before we begin would any of you like a drink?'

All three of them asked for a coffee which Grace asked an intern to fetch for them.

Grace started by telling them the plan for the afternoon.

'So, once we are finished, you'll meet with the President, the Directors of the CIA, FBI, NSA and the Head of the Secret Service,' she said.

'How come we are meeting the Heads of so many different agencies?' asked Alex.

'Yes, I thought we were working for the Secret Service,' added Riley.

'You are,' said Grace, 'but as the President will explain in more detail, your role will be far wider than that of any Secret Service agent.'

'In what way?' asked Casey.

'I'll let the President explain, but it will involve an

unprecedented level of interagency cooperation, hence the fact you're meeting everyone today.'

Riley, Casey and Alex looked at each other. Grace could tell they were feeling anxious.

'There's nothing to worry about,' she said. 'We will look after you.'

She could see the three of them were still worrying so she decided to move the conversation onto the next topic.

'I expect you have lots of questions,' she said, 'let's see if I can answer some of them now.'

Riley raised her hand a little to get Grace's attention. 'Yes,' said Grace.

'If we are here for three months, where will be living, as I'm guessing the government aren't putting us up in a hotel all that time?'

'No, they're not,' replied Grace, 'instead they're putting you in a house together in Arlington, just over the Potomac.'

'That's great,' said Riley; 'my next question was would we be together?'

Grace smiled. She was pleased to see their faces becoming a little more relaxed.

'Here's your coffees,' said the intern, coming into the room carrying a tray.

'Thanks,' replied Riley.

'None of us have ever run a home before, so what do we do about money, shopping, cooking and so on?' asked Casey.

'Good question,' said Grace. 'That's all taken care of. You'll have a housekeeper living nearby. She will do your shopping and cooking and look after the house. That will free you up to study and train for the Secret Service.'

'Thanks, that sounds great,' said Casey.

'That was going to be my next question,' said Alex; 'What's happening about our school and college studies?'

'Okay,' said Grace, taking a deep breath, 'you'll all study at home. Every morning a specialist tutor will come to work with you, Alex, so you can keep up with your course. The girls will be tutored together by someone else as they are still in high school. The afternoons will be spent training.'

'What about our cover story with our families?' asked Casey.

'Yeah, they think we are Youth Ambassadors going into schools,' added Riley.

'Yes, and you'll do some of that so that you have things to tell your parents and pictures to send,' said Grace.

Just as she finished speaking an aide opened the door.

'The President would like to see them now,' he said.

'Very well,' said Grace. She got up from her seat and said: 'Follow me, please.'

Riley, Casey and Alex got up, pushed their chairs neatly back under the table and followed Grace out of the room. They walked along a busy corridor towards the Oval Office. Grace knocked, then opened the door.

'Mr President,' she said.

'Ah, here we are,' replied the President, 'come in, you three. Thanks, Grace.'

'No problem, sir,' said Grace as she left, closing the door behind her.

The three of them made their way into the Oval Office. There were a number of smartly dressed adults standing around waiting to meet them.

'This is Riley, Casey and Alex,' said the President. They each said hello and in turn the various Agency Directors were introduced. 'Hi, I'm Jack Andrews, Director of the Secret Service and I will be your Line Manager. These are my colleagues, Director Helen Charleston from the NSA, Director Rohan Montgomery from the CIA and Director Luca Jackson from the FBI.' Once everyone was introduced, they all sat down.

'Okay,' said the President, 'as you all know, I don't normally involve myself quite so directly with Agency operations; however, this is different. These three young people have unique skills which I believe would be of benefit to you all. I also believe their involvement in the Secret Service will require closer interagency cooperation.'

The President paused and looked at Riley. 'Riley, would you mind demonstrating your gift to everyone here?'

'Of course, sir,' she replied. She grabbed Casey's hand as she got up. 'Can you catch me?' she said quietly.

'Of course,' said Casey following her onto the carpet in front of the President's desk.

Riley stretched out her arms and started to spin. Round and round she went until the brain burn started in her head. Casey ran forward to catch her as she started to fall. But, for those watching, Riley was gone. Casey was standing holding thin air as far as they could tell. As the burning passed Riley said, 'I'm okay now.' Casey let go and went to sit down.

'So, where is she?' said Rohan, the CIA Director.

'Watch the President's desk,' said Alex.

They all watched as the President's chair moved, then the pen on his desk stood up and made its way across the desk.

'Impressive,' said Luca, the FBI Director.

The President turned to Alex and asked, 'Where is she now?'

Alex replied, 'Look at your tie, sir.'

The President looked down to see his tie pulled out straight in front of him and slowly rising until it sat horizontally in mid-air.

'Well done, Riley,' said the President. 'Can you rejoin us now?'

Casey got up again and this time everyone saw Riley as Casey caught her at the end of her spin. Once her brain burn had gone, she sat back on the sofa next to Casey and Alex.

'I can see why you wanted these three working for the Secret Service,' said Rohan.

'So can I,' said Luca, 'but what is it you think they can do?'

'Well,' said the President, 'you know how they prevented my assassination and you've all read their files, and so know the other things they've done.'

'Yes, sir, we do,' said Helen.

'With the correct training I think the three of them could be a huge asset to the country, both domestically and abroad. Imagine an asset that no-one can see, except her team. Imagine the lives she could save; the terror attacks she could stop before they start.'

'We all agree, sir,' said Rohan, 'but they are just kids and younger than any agent any of us has ever recruited.'

'I hear what you're saying,' said the President, 'but that's also what makes them perfect for this, because no-one would expect three teenagers to be trained field agents.'

'Sir, if I may,' said Riley.

'Of course,' said the President.

'We recognise this is outside normal protocol for you all, but it is for us too,' she said. 'However, we believe with your help we can make a difference.'

The Directors still looked a little sceptical.

'Sir, can I have your help for a minute?' said Riley to the President.

'By all means,' he replied. They both stood up and Riley led him to the carpet in the middle of the Oval Office.

'Do you trust me, sir?' she said.

'Completely,' replied the President.

Riley backed several metres away from him. Alex and Casey were staring at her, wondering what she was planning.

'Okay, sir,' said Riley, 'on the count of three I want you to fall forwards on the carpet.' The President's protection detail stepped forward from the doors where they were standing.

'It's okay,' said the President, signalling for them to stand down. 'Very well,' he said to Riley.

Riley counted, and as she said 'three,' the President threw himself towards the floor in front of her. Much to the amazement of everyone in the room, including her friends, the President never landed. Riley had put up her hand and released an energy pulse from it. It had caught the President as he fell and she was now using the pulse to gently stand him upright on the floor.

'Incredible,' said Luca.

'And this is what you used to save thirty girls in your school from a collapsing roof?' asked Helen.

'Yes, ma'am,' said Riley.

Casey gave Riley a little pat of the back as she and the President sat back down.

'Very well,' said Rohan, 'the CIA and the Secret Service will work together to provide training for the three of you. We will then work with any agency required for the assignments the Secret Service wish to involve Riley and her team in.'

'Excellent,' said the President. Turning to Riley, Casey and Alex, the President said, 'Grace will arrange to take you to Arlington now so you can settle into your new home. Then tomorrow you'll meet your tutors in the morning and spend the afternoon with the CIA at Langley.'

'Yes, sir,' they replied. Everyone stood as the three of them were led out of the Oval Office.

'How did that go?' asked Grace as she led them to her office.

'Very well, thanks,' said Riley.

'Take a seat for a minute while I arrange for someone to take you to Arlington,' said Grace.

The three of them sat down.

'Wow, Riley, when did you learn to control the energy pulse like that?' asked Casey.

'Well I've had some free time these last few weeks so I thought I'd put it to good use,' replied Riley, smiling.

Moments later the agent who'd collected them from the airport appeared.

'You guys ready to go?' he said.

They got up and followed him back to the 4x4 in the car park, climbing back into the same seats. The car pulled out of the White House grounds and headed through the streets of Washington towards the Potomac River and Arlington.

Chapter 5

Arlington

Everyone was very quiet in the car. They all needed time to process what was happening. After all, it was only 24 hours since they were sitting in the cafe by the library drinking milkshakes. They all stared out of the window watching life go by as the car wound through the city streets and onto the bridge across the Potomac River.

Finally, the car pulled up outside a house in a suburban street in Lee Heights, Arlington.

'Here we are,' said Agent Jacobs, as he handed Riley a set of keys. 'This is your place.'

They looked through the car window at the house. It was a red brick building with black shutters on the sash windows. The short path led to a black front door surrounded by a white porch.

As they got out of the car, Agent Jacobs said he'd pick them up tomorrow afternoon to go to Langley. They made their way up the path, carrying their bags. As they reached the door, it opened. Standing on the step was a woman wearing an apron.

'Hello, come in, my name is Elsie and I'll be looking after you during your stay in Arlington,' she said.

They each said hello and introduced themselves as they went in.

Inside there was a broad staircase that led to the first floor and to the right of it a corridor that led to the lounge, a study and kitchen/diner.

'If you go upstairs,' said Elsie, 'you'll find two bedrooms at the front of the house and a bedroom and bathroom at the back. I'll let you settle in. Come and join me in the kitchen when you're ready and I'll go through dinner options with you.'

'Thank you, Elsie,' said Riley, as she and the others

made their way upstairs.

At the top of the stairs, Alex asked, 'Any preference on rooms?'

'I don't mind,' said Riley.

'Why don't Riley and I take the front rooms and you take the back?' said Casey.

'Fine by me,' said Alex, walking towards the back room.

Each room was laid out in a similar way. It had a large bed with a bedside table, wardrobe, chest of draws and a free-standing mirror. The decor was a little old fashioned for Riley's taste, but the place felt homely, which was what she needed right now.

Placing her bags on the bed she opened the larger one and started to take out the clothes. She spent some time placing everything neatly in drawers and on hangers in her wardrobe.

'Hey there,' said Casey, sticking her head round the door. 'How are you getting on?'

'Oh, fine,' replied Riley, 'how about you?'

'I'm all done,' said Casey, coming into the room and sitting down on Riley's bed.

Riley closed her empty bag and placed it on top of her wardrobe.

'Shall we go downstairs? I'm feeling pretty hungry,' she asked Riley.

'Fine by me,' said Casey. They called for Alex on the way. He too had unpacked everything and put it away.

They made their way back downstairs and went through to the kitchen. There they found Elsie busy sorting through bags of shopping.

'Do you need a hand with that?' asked Riley.

'Oh, it's okay, dear. I'll sort this. You take a seat,' said Elsie. They all sat down round the kitchen table.

'Now,' said Elsie, 'tell me: what would you three like for dinner tonight?'

They looked at each other and almost at the same time they all said 'burgers, please!'

Elsie smiled. 'Very well, I'll get that sorted for you. Feel free to relax, make a drink, watch TV. This is your home now.'

'Thanks, Elsie,' said Alex. 'Coffee anyone?' Alex got up and went to put the kettle on.

'Yes, please,' replied Riley.

'I'm okay for now, thanks,' said Casey.

Once the drinks were made, they went through to the lounge. It was quite cosy, with a two-seater sofa and an armchair. The sofa was one of those with a button on the side. Press it and your legs are lifted off the ground. There was a television in the room and some books on a bookcase. The room had some pictures of the Blue Ridge Mountains on the walls.

Alex sat down in the armchair, leaving the sofa for the girls.

'I wonder what our tutors will be like tomorrow,' said Casey.

'Yeah, it's gonna be weird being home schooled after being in high school for so many years,' said Riley.

'I just hope my tutor knows his stuff,' said Alex.

'I'm sure he will,' said Riley. 'They seem to have gone to great lengths to organise all this for us.'

They spent the evening at the house. Elsie called them through to the kitchen to eat the home-made burgers she'd cooked for them.

'If there's nothing else you need from me, I'll be heading home,' she said.

'Are you not staying here?' asked Riley, forgetting there were only three bedrooms upstairs.

'No, dear, but if you have any problems call me. I only live three doors down.'

'Thanks, Elsie,' said Riley.

'Thanks for the burgers too. They were awesome,' said Casey.

'My pleasure, dear,' replied Elsie, 'I'll see you in the morning.' With that, she left the house.

Riley, Casey and Alex spent the rest of the evening talking in the lounge. They each took it in turns to contact their parents and share what little they could about their day. Around 11 p.m. Alex suggested they go to bed as the coming days and weeks would be tiring. The girls agreed. Everyone made their way up to their rooms and said goodnight before going their separate ways. Riley went into her room, closing the door behind her. She took off her clothes and put on her pyjama shorts and vest top. Before getting into bed she decided to brush her teeth.

Heading back out of her room, she found Casey standing there in her nightie; it was plain, dark blue with straps over the shoulders.

'Are you waiting for Alex to get out of the bathroom?' asked Riley.

'Yeah, join the queue,' said Casey, 'we could be here a while!'

'I heard that!' said Alex from inside the bathroom.

The girls both laughed. Alex finally emerged and Casey went in. She wasn't there for too long, which meant Riley could get her teeth cleaned and get to bed.

Riley woke early the next day to hear Elsie talking to Alex in the kitchen. Bleary-eyed, she got out of bed. Unsure where she'd put her slippers, she went barefoot downstairs.

'Morning, sleepyhead,' said Casey as Riley entered the kitchen.

'Have I overslept?' she asked, rubbing her eyes.

'No,' replied Alex, 'the rest of us were just up early, that's all. Do you want a coffee?'

'Yes, please,' replied Riley as she collapsed into a chair at the kitchen table.

'Did everyone sleep well?' asked Elsie as she put some eggs and bacon into a frying pan.

'Yes, thanks,' they each replied in turn.

After Elsie had served them breakfast, she reminded them that their tutors would be arriving in an hour. Fortunately, Casey and Alex had already showered, leaving the bathroom free for Riley. The others helped Elsie clear away as Riley made her way back upstairs to have a shower.

When she reappeared, the tutors were arriving at the

house.

'I suggest you use the study, Alex, and the girls work at the kitchen table,' said Elsie.

'Fine by me,' said Alex as he and his tutor went through to the study to get started.

The girls sat at the kitchen table looking at the tutor who had come to teach them.

'I'll leave you to it,' said Elsie. 'I'll be back later to sort your lunch.'

'Thanks, Elsie,' said Riley.

'Well, good morning, you two,' said the tutor, 'my name is Mrs Jordan and I'll be your tutor for the next three months.'

During the course of the morning, Riley, Casey and Alex went through the work they'd covered so far on their courses. The tutors set out a plan for each of them, for work they'd cover in the next three months. If they could stick to this with all the other things they'd be doing, then they would stay on track with their peers back home.

They were all relieved when 12 o'clock came and the lessons finished. The tutors had decided to go easy on them for the first day and not set any homework.

'We'll see you tomorrow,' said Mrs Jordan as she and Alex's tutor left the house.

Elsie was busy in the kitchen making some soup and sandwiches for them.

'Do you know what time we are being picked up?' asked Riley.

'I think it's around 1.00 p.m., dear,' replied Elsie.

They sat at the kitchen table eating the vegetable soup and cheese sandwiches Elsie had made for them.

'How was your tutor?' asked Alex.

'Good, thanks,' said Casey; 'glad she didn't set any homework, though.'

'How about yours?' asked Riley.

'Really good, actually,' replied Alex, 'he knew his stuff and get this, his name is Rex. I so wanted to call him T-Rex.' Riley laughed.

'Why's that funny?' asked Casey.

'Because he's a dinosaur specialist,' said Alex, shaking his head.

Once they'd finished lunch, they all got changed into their sports clothes. The girls put on sports bra tops and tracksuit bottoms with a hoodie. Alex had a vest top, tracksuit bottoms and a hoodie. They'd all been sent a text telling them what to wear ready for their first training session at Langley.

'I'm guessing today is physical training,' said Casey.

'Yeah, I expect they'll want to see what our fitness level is like and decide what they need to work on with us,' said Alex.

Soon after they'd all changed, the doorbell rang. They opened it to find Agent Jacobs standing there.

'You three ready to go?' he said.

Chapter 6

The CIA

Riley, Casey and Alex got into the Secret Service 4x4 and put their seat belts on. Agent Jacobs did the same, then turned on the ignition.

'Okay, let's do this,' said Agent Jacobs. With that he put his foot on the gas and off they went in the direction of Langley and the Central Intelligence Agency.

It took no time at all to reach the CIA Headquarters. On arrival they each passed through stringent security checks. They were scanned and patted down by a security guard. They had to empty their pockets so everything could be X-rayed. Once inside they were met by Jack from the Secret Service and James, the CIA agent who had carried out their induction as Special Agents.

'Good afternoon,' said Jack, 'welcome to the CIA. If you'd like to follow us, we will take you to a briefing room to go through everything with you.'

The three friends went through several corridors and up a level to an area of the building they'd not been in before.

'Here we are,' said James, opening a door, 'come in and take a seat.'

There was a large round table in the room with six chairs at it. They all filed in and sat down. Jack and James joined them.

'Okay,' said Jack, 'let's get started.'

James took point in the conversation from there, as he explained what the next three months would entail.

'We are going to carry out a physical assessment on each of you. You'll have tests for various illnesses and conditions,' he said.

'What sort of tests?' asked Riley.

'Blood tests and scans,' said James.

'Oh,' said Riley, 'we are all used to those.'

'We will also carry out physical and psychological training with you – including teaching you martial arts as a form of self-defence.'

'That sounds good,' said Casey.

'It'll be tough,' said Jack. 'This training will be the same as we do for other recruits who are all in their twenties or older. You three are the youngest team we've ever worked with.'

'What else will we be learning?' asked Riley.

'You'll learn some of the basic analytic skills required to gather good intelligence, along with the investigative skills required by agents working in the field,' said James.

'Sounds like a lot to take in,' said Alex.

'It is,' said James, 'but don't worry, we will help you through it.'

After their briefing Jack said goodbye and left them with James for the afternoon. He took them to the medical centre on site for some tests and then to the gym.

'Okay guys, we are going to do a series of fitness tests this afternoon so we can provide you each with a training programme to follow,' said James.

In the gym, they each took turns to run on a treadmill, lift weights, do core exercises etc. Everything was recorded.

'Okay, take ten minutes before we go to the martial arts training room,' said James.

The three of them sat on a bench in the corner of the gym, sweat rolling down their faces. They'd all taken off their hoodies in an attempt to cool down.

'I'm shattered,' said Riley.

'Me too!' said Casey.

'I have a feeling we are just getting started,' said Alex.

The girls looked at him, knowing he was right but wishing he wasn't. They each drank an entire bottle of water before James reappeared.

'Come on, you three,' said James, 'no rest for the wicked!'

They each forced their muscles to respond and got up from the bench. James led them along the corridor to a nearby gym which had matting across the entire floor. Once inside they met with Koba, a Japanese martial arts specialist.

'Guys, this is Koba, he's one of our top agents and a master in several martial arts. He's going to conduct this part of your training. I'll call back for you later,' said James.

'Come in, guys, and put your shoes and socks over by the bench, please,' said Koba.

They all placed their hoodies on the bench and put their shoes and socks underneath before standing in a circle in the centre of the gym with Koba.

'Today I'm going to introduce you to a mixture of different martial arts,' said Koba. 'We will focus on defensive moves today. Okay, so who would like to go first?' he added.

'I will,' said Riley.

She'd become more and more confident since the lightning strike and was often the one to go first now.

'Very well,' said Koba, 'raise your arms like this.' He crossed his arms into an X and put them out in front of his chest; Riley did the same.

'From here you can move your body to defend from either side; watch,' he said as he demonstrated the next movement.

For the rest of the session, the girls worked together and Alex and Koba paired up. Koba took them through a series of movements which allowed them to grasp the basics.

'Over the coming months I will develop your skills so you can handle yourselves in a fight without causing harm to your opponents,' he said.

'Don't we want to cause them harm?' asked Casey.

'No,' said Koba, 'your job is to neutralise them so they can be detained and interrogated.'

'Ah, yeah, that makes sense,' replied Casey.

'Okay, this is enough for today,' said Koba.

They stood back in the circle and finished with a small bow before going to the bench to put their shoes and socks back on.

James reappeared as they were putting hoodies on.

'Ready to head back to Arlington?' he asked.

'Definitely,' said Alex. 'I think we are all exhausted.'

'Well, get an early night,' said James, 'because you've got more of the same tomorrow!'

They left the gym and James took them back to the main entrance, where Agent Jacobs was waiting for them. They were all very quiet in the car going back to the house in Arlington.

'Tough day?' asked Agent Jacobs.

'Very,' said Riley.

'Better get used to that,' said Agent Jacobs.

No-one responded but they were all thinking the same – *How on earth are we gonna get through this?*

Once through the front door they all went straight to the lounge and collapsed on the sofa. Elsie came through from the kitchen.

'Are you all okay?' she asked.

'Yes, thanks, Elsie, just really tired,' replied Casey.

'Well why don't you each have a shower and put your PJs on and I'll sort you some dinner.'

'Thanks, Elsie, that's a great idea,' said Alex.

'Who wants to go first?' asked Casey.

'I'm happy to,' said Riley pushing herself off the sofa and onto her tired legs.

'Okay, but don't take forever,' said Alex.

'Oh, that's rich coming from you,' said Riley, laughing.

Riley climbed the stairs slowly. Every step was a challenge. It was only a staircase, but it might as well have been the death zone on Mount Everest when it came to the effort involved to reach the top. Finally, she made it to her room and grabbed her towel. She went into the bathroom and locked the door. Taking off her sportswear she stepped into the shower cubicle and closed the screen. She turned on the water. It felt so good as it flowed over her skin. Although it was hot water it still seemed to feel cool on the aching muscles in her body. She didn't take too long as the others needed to do the same before dinner. When she'd finished, she shouted 'bathroom's free,' so the next person could get started.

Once they were all showered, and in their pyjamas, Riley, Casey and Alex went and sat at the kitchen table and talked to Elsie as she cooked their tea for them.

'What's on the menu today?' asked Casey.

'Spaghetti,' replied Elsie.

'Great,' said Casey, 'one of our favourites.'

They were all quite quiet at dinner, most likely due to the exhaustion taking hold of each of them. After dinner, Elsie made them each a hot drink before leaving them for the night.

It could only have been 8.30 p.m. when Alex announced: 'I'm off to bed.' The girls didn't seem surprised by this as they both wanted to go to sleep as well.

'Let's get an early night,' said Riley.

'Good idea,' said Casey.

All three made their way to the top of the stairs, gave each other a goodnight hug and went to their rooms. No-one reappeared to use the bathroom or clean teeth as they had all crashed out on their beds as soon as they'd entered their rooms.

'Beep, beep, beep' went Riley's alarm. She reached out from under the bed sheets and hit it to silence it. *It can't be morning already,* she thought to herself. But sure enough, daylight was coming through the sash window, finding the little gaps in the curtains. Yawning, she stretched her arms and pulled back the covers. Swinging her legs out of bed, she put her bare feet onto the carpet. It felt cold compared to the warmth of the bed. She got up and made her way to the bathroom. Sometime later, she appeared downstairs dressed in her sports gear again.

'Morning, dear,' said Elsie as Riley sat down at the kitchen table.

The others drifted in behind her, saying 'good morning' as they came into the kitchen. Once everyone was there, Elsie served breakfast. She'd cooked some eggs and toast which everyone tucked into. All three of them had realised very quickly that eating food would give them the energy they'd need to get through the training. They also realised they would soon burn it off once training started.

The morning was spent with their tutors once again. Soon after lunch the doorbell rang and Agent Jacobs was there to take them back to Langley. Training consisted of more of the same with Koba. As before, they were instructed to put their shoes and socks by the bench. They all took off their hoodies as well. If yesterday's training had only taught them one thing, it was that it would be a hot and tiring few hours.

Riley enjoyed the session more today. Koba introduced some new elements to their training, including how to take down an opponent. By the end of the session, Riley had managed to throw Casey over her shoulder. She also took Alex down by blocking his attack while taking his legs out from under him.

'You have a natural talent for this, Riley,' said Koba.

'Thanks,' said Riley, trying not to blush.

'Tomorrow I will ask you each to deal with two opponents attacking at once. It will be an interesting session.'

The three of them looked at each other, but said nothing. Clearly Koba had a different definition of interesting to them.

'I'm up for the challenge,' said Riley in a tired but upbeat voice.

'Very well,' said Koba, 'that is all for today.'

They formed the circle and bowed to their instructor before going to put their shoes back on.

After martial arts training, they spent an hour with James, who started to teach them some of the intelligence gathering skills they'd need. As they left with Agent Jacobs, they discussed that final hour in the car.

'I'm not sure how ploughing through telephone records or bank statements helps us stop bad guys,' said Casey, who had found James's lesson a struggle.

Agent Jacobs interjected. 'It helps you understand what

a bad guy, as you put it, has been up to,' he said.

'I guess it would then help us understand what he might do next,' added Riley.

'Yeah,' said Agent Jacobs, 'that's exactly it.' Riley smiled.

'I understand,' said Casey, 'it's just not what you see on the movies.'

'Intelligence work very rarely is,' said Agent Jacobs.

Their training continued for several weeks with physical exercise, martial arts and various analytical skills. They also spent several days at FBI Headquarters in Washington DC. There, agents helped them to learn basic investigative skills. It was a huge amount to take in. As the weeks went by, they grew stronger and started to understand just how diverse their role would ultimately be.

'They're going to have us saving the world at this rate,' said Casey, jokingly.

'You may joke now,' said Alex, 'but I think there's more truth in that comment than you know!'

Chapter 7

Take-Off

Riley came into the kitchen wearing a dressing gown and rubbing her hair with a towel.

'Morning, guys,' she said.

'Morning,' replied Casey and Alex.

'I can't believe we've got a rest day!' said Riley.

'Yeah,' said Alex, 'took three weeks but we finally got one!'

'So, what are we gonna do?' said Casey.

'No idea,' replied Alex.

'I'm easy as long as it's fun and doesn't involve too much effort,' said Riley. She put the kettle on to make some coffee. 'Any ideas?' she added.

Casey and Alex looked at each other. They'd all been in such a strict routine of training that they'd almost forgotten what to do to relax. Riley finally broke the silence as she poured coffee into cups for the three of them. Sitting down she said, 'How about swimming?'

'I guess we could do,' said Alex.

'I'm up for that,' said Casey, 'we could go somewhere for lunch afterwards.'

'That's a nice idea,' said Riley.

After breakfast they got ready to go and set off for the Yorktown Aquatic Centre. It wasn't too busy as their rest day was mid-week so people were in work and school. The result was they more or less had the place to themselves. Once they were changed into their swimsuits the girls went through to the pool area and found Alex already in the water. Jumping in they resurfaced near him and swam over.

'Hey, you fancy a race?' said Riley.

'I thought this was meant to be relaxing?' said Alex smiling.

'Come on,' added Casey, 'it'll be fun.'

Alex knew he wasn't going to win this argument so he gave in and the three of them swam to the shallow end of the pool.

'Okay,' said Riley, 'to the end and back. First one is the winner.' She counted to three and they set off.

They all reached the deep end around the same time but it was Casey who took the lead on the way back, beating the others by a few metres.

'Hey, well done,' said Alex.

'I wonder if I could go faster in the water if I used my energy pulse,' said Riley.

'You just wanna beat me,' said Casey.

'True,' replied Riley, 'but it would be interesting to know.'

'Why don't you try it?' said Alex. 'Keep an arm in front of you so you don't crash your head at the end of the pool.'

'I've a better idea,' said Casey. 'I'll go to the other end to help stop you if needed.'

'Thanks, Casey,' said Riley. They waited while Casey swam to the far end of the pool.

'Try and control the energy like you did with the President,' said Alex.

'I will,' said Riley as she got into position in the water.

Placing one arm in front and the other pointing back towards her feet she focused. Suddenly, she shot forward in the water, leaving a wake behind her. It only took a few seconds to reach Casey, who barely had time to raise her hands before Riley came crashing into her.

'You two okay?' shouted Alex as he started to swim towards them.

By the time he arrived the girls were laughing. Casey had caught Riley but the force had pushed them both against the side of the pool.

'You alright?' asked Alex.

'Yeah we're fine,' said Casey.

Alex paused for a moment.

'What is it, Alex?' asked Riley, 'I can tell there's some sort of theory going around in that brain of yours.'

'There is,' said Alex. The girls listened as Alex talked through the idea he was having.

'So, you're saying if I can use the pulse to move through water, I could use it to move through the air,' said Riley.

'I think it's a possibility,' said Alex, 'one we should explore.'

'Hold on, are you talking about flying like Superman?' said Casey.

'Not exactly,' said Alex. 'The energy pulse moved her in the water because it pushed her away from the side of the pool.'

'So as long as the pulse was pointing at a solid object, such as the ground, it could push me in the opposite direction,' said Riley.

'Potentially,' replied Alex.

'Why don't we test that here?' suggested Riley, 'if it goes wrong, I'll just fall back into the water.'

'Good idea,' said Alex.

'Look, I don't want to put a dampener on this but what about the lifeguard at the side of the pool?' said Casey.

'Oh yeah, good call,' said Alex.

'No problem, I'll go into the changing area and spin invisible,' said Riley.

The girls went together as Riley would need Casey to hold her until the brain burn subsided. They re-emerged a few minutes later and jumped back into the water. Moving to a deeper part of the pool, the three of them trod water.

'Okay, Riley, we'll back up and give you some space. You'll have to be careful. If you use too much energy you'll smash into the roof!' said Alex.

'Good point,' said Riley, looking up at the metal beams.

As the others swam away a little, Riley put both arms down by her sides with her palms pointing towards the bottom of the pool. As she concentrated, the energy pulse began to push her up out of the water. The others watched as she rose into the air. Suddenly she lost her control and fell, with a splash, back into the water. The others swam back to her as fast as they could.

'You okay?' asked Casey as Riley resurfaced from the bottom of the pool.

'Yeah, I'm fine,' replied Riley.

'That was amazing,' said Alex.

'Yeah, it was but I need to be able to lower myself too. I can't go taking off with no way to land safely,' replied Riley.

'Why don't you try again?' suggested Casey.

They moved back to the same positions so Riley could try again. This time she went more slowly and was able to lift herself higher in the air above the pool. She hovered there for a moment before lowering herself back to the water, this time re-entering the pool without making a splash. The others swam back in and gave her a hug in the water.

'That's incredible,' said Casey.

'Yeah, it is. We need to see if she can do it on dry ground now,' said Alex.

'Okay,' said Riley, 'but let's get changed and have some lunch first, eh!'

The three of them swam to the side and got out of the pool. They met up in the centre reception half an hour later and headed out to find a diner for some lunch.

'You know you're still invisible,' said Alex to Riley.

'Yeah, I know,' said Riley, 'I'll have to spin back in the bathroom at the diner.' It didn't take them long to find a place to stop.

'I'll order while you two sort Riley out,' said Alex. 'I presume everyone wants burgers.'

'You know us too well,' replied Casey as the girls headed off to the bathroom.

By the time they reappeared Alex was at the table with drinks sorted.

'I got you two milkshakes as I figured you'd want the extra sugar with all the exercise we do these days,' he said.

'Thanks,' said Riley, sitting down opposite him.

'So where are we going to do the dry land flight test?' said Casey, sitting next to her.

'We could go to Chestnut Hills Park,' said Alex, 'I saw a sign for it as we left the aquatic centre so it can't be far.'

The waitress came over with their burgers.

'Thanks for these,' said Riley to Alex.

'No problem,' he replied as he took a large bite.

Once they were finished, they left the diner and walked back towards the aquatic centre.

'There!' shouted Casey with some excitement.

The others looked and, sure enough, the park was just across the way.

'Okay,' said Riley, 'let's find a secluded spot for me to spin invisible.'

They made their way into the park and found a wooded area.

'This will do,' said Riley, putting down her swim bag.

They were surrounded by trees and there was no-one else around.

'Okay,' said Alex, 'we're ready when you are.'

Riley began to spin round and round. As she spun faster her body matched the speed of the energy in her brain. At that moment a burning sensation filled her head.

'The brain burn,' said Casey as she and Alex put their arms out to stop Riley falling over. A few moments later Riley's head had cleared.

'I'm okay, guys. You can let go now,' she said.

They found a small clearing in the park away from the children's playground. It was at the east side of the park near some open fields.

'This will be perfect,' said Riley.

'Okay,' said Alex, 'remember, slow and gentle. You need to control your descent.'

'I know,' replied Riley, feeling a little patronised. She ignored the feeling as she knew Alex was just looking out for her safety.

Alex and Casey stepped back to give Riley some room. Just as she'd done in the swimming pool, she put her arms by her side with her palms facing the ground. As she focused, the energy pulse from her hands pushed her off the ground and into the air. She rose up and up until she was level with the tree tops.

'Okay,' shouted Casey, 'that'll do.'

Clearly worried her friend would be injured, Casey had run back to where Riley had taken off from. As Riley descended back to the ground, she noticed Casey below her. Thinking quickly, she changed the angle of her hands to move sideways in the air and avoid landing on her friend.

'Wow,' said Alex, 'that was close.'

'It was, but it's shown us something new,' said Riley. 'I can move around while I'm in the air.'

'Sorry,' said Casey, 'I didn't mean to get in the way.'

'No, it's okay,' said Riley, 'I'm glad you did. Alex, I want to try something.'

'What's that, Riley?' he asked.

'Flight!' she replied. The others looked at her with stunned expressions.

'Just across this clearing,' she replied. 'I'm not taking off to New York!'

The others agreed and went to the south end of the clearing. Riley went to the north. Once there, she did the same as before, but this time stayed lower to the ground; angling the palms of her hands, she increased the energy pulse. The extra force pushed her through the air towards Casey and Alex. As she got closer, she reduced the pulse and her speed. She came into land a few feet in front of them. Casey ran forward to hug her friend.

'That was truly amazing,' she said while she was holding Riley close.

'Nice one,' said Alex.

'Thanks,' said Riley, 'it needs some work.'

'Yeah, but even so, you can fly!' replied Alex.

'I can fly!' said Riley, suddenly realising what she'd just achieved.

'I guess we'd better tell Director Andrews when we next see him,' said Alex.

'Yeah, I'll try and practice a bit before that,' said Riley.

They made their way back to Lee Heights, finding a

coffee shop on the way. Riley had made herself visible again while they were in the park. As they sat drinking coffee they had loads to talk about.

'I wonder how fast you can move,' said Casey.

'Or how high I can go,' added Riley.

'I guess we can test these things,' said Alex, 'but it may be safer to do so with the help of the Secret Service.'

'You're probably right,' said Riley.

When they reached the house, they found Elsie inside, busy making dinner in the kitchen.

'Hey Elsie, how are you?' said Riley.

'I'm well, thanks,' she replied. 'Have you had a good day today?'

'We have, thanks,' said Alex.

'We've been swimming and to the park,' added Casey.

'Sounds fun,' said Elsie. 'Dinner will be about an hour, so I'd give your parents a call while you wait.'

Chapter 8

NASA

That evening they each called home to catch up with their parents before sitting down for dinner. They spent the evening watching television before getting to bed around 11.00 p.m.

'We'd better not stay up any later as it's back to training in the morning,' said Alex.

The next day Agent Jacobs took them to Langley as usual. They were dressed in their sports gear and ready for another gruelling training session with Koba. Before any of the training began, they ran into Director Jack Andrews from the Secret Service.

'Morning, sir,' said Alex.

'Oh, hello, you three. How's the training going?' asked Jack.

'It's tough, sir, but we are doing fine,' said Casey.

'Sir, I'm glad we've run into you as I need to share something important with you,' said Riley.

'Oh, what is it?' said Jack.

'Can we go somewhere other than this corridor to speak?' asked Riley.

'Yes, of course,' said Jack, looking around for an empty office.

'Here,' he said, opening a nearby door. They followed Jack into the office and closed the door.

'Now tell me, what is this important news?' asked Jack.

'I can fly, sir,' said Riley.

'You can what?' said Jack.

'Fly, sir,' repeated Riley.

'Yes, yes I heard you the first time,' said Jack sitting down at the empty desk in the office. 'Well, this changes things a bit,' he added. 'When did you discover this?'

'Yesterday at the aquatic centre and later in the park,'

said Riley.

'How?' said Jack sounding a little bewildered.

'The energy pulse, the one I used to stop the President from falling over in the Oval Office. Well if I direct it down to the ground with enough force it lifts me into the air.'

With that she stood away from the others, put her arms by her side and very gently lifted off the ground just a little. She moved her palms slightly and glided across the room, crashing into a filing cabinet.

Alex ran over to help her back onto her feet.

'Well, it needs some work,' said Riley brushing herself down as she stood back up.

'This is amazing,' said Jack, 'and I know just the people to help you develop this skill to perfection. How would you like a trip to NASA?'

On hearing those words Alex nearly collapsed with excitement. He was a space geek and had been so thrilled to visit the National Air and Space Museum in Washington after they'd saved the President.

'That would be awesome,' said Alex.

'What exactly can NASA do for Riley?' asked Casey.

'They have a huge dome at the Kennedy Space Centre in Florida. I'll contact their Director about you using it. I know they've been working with the Air Force to develop anti-gravity flight suits. Leave this with me for an hour, will you?'

'Of course, sir,' said Riley.

Riley, Casey and Alex made their way to the canteen for a drink, while Director Andrews made some calls to NASA and the Air Force.

'NASA,' said Alex sounding as if he'd just fallen in love. The girls laughed.

'Alex, get a grip,' said Casey.

'Hey, leave him alone. He's allowed to be excited if he wants,' said Riley.

'Thanks, Riley,' said Alex. 'Just like the Air and Space Museum, the Kennedy Space Centre is somewhere I've always wanted to see.'

'Well I suspect you'll get your wish if Director Andrews has anything to do with it,' said Casey.

Just as they finished their drinks, the Director arrived in the canteen.

'There you are,' he said. 'I've arranged for the three of you to spend two days in Florida. There's a plane at Reagan National waiting for you. When you get there ask for Air Force Commander Adams.'

'Yes, sir,' replied Riley.

The three of them set off with Agent Jacobs to the airport. They called at the house to grab overnight bags. A little over an hour later they were sitting on a private jet heading for Orlando Airport in Florida.

'I still can't believe we are on our way to the Kennedy Space Centre and all because we decided to have a race in the swimming pool yesterday which resulted in you flying,' said Alex.

'Yeah, when you put it like that it is a little crazy,' said Riley.

'Well we've got over five hours until we get there so I'm gonna take a nap,' said Alex.

'Okay,' said Riley, taking her sketch pad out of her bag, 'I'm going to take the opportunity to do some artwork as we never get a block of time like this on a normal day.'

'We never get a normal day,' added Casey, looking up from a book she'd brought with her.

The flight went more quickly than they'd expected and it wasn't long before they were disembarking in Orlando. An official from NASA met them to take them to the Kennedy Space Centre.

'Is this your first time to NASA?' she asked.

'It's my first time to Florida!' replied Casey.

'Well I hope you enjoy your visit,' said the official.

They were met at the main entrance by a woman in an Air Force uniform.

'Commander Adams?' asked Alex in a questioning tone.

'I am,' came the reply. 'Welcome to NASA.'

'Thank you,' said Alex.

'Now which one of you is Riley Bennett?' asked Commander Adams.

'I am,' said Riley.

'Nice to meet you,' said the Commander. She shook hands with all three of them and then asked them to follow her inside.

In yet another briefing room the three teenagers sat with Commander Adams and NASA pilot Harrison. Riley told them about her energy pulse and what she could do with it. The Commander then talked to them about the highly classified development programme NASA and the US Air Force were working on together.

'So, let me get this right,' said Casey, 'these are personal flight suits that don't require a plane.'

'Yes, Casey,' said Harrison, 'they work in a similar way to Riley's energy pulse, but have micro jets in various parts of the suit to control movement.'

'Director Andrews sent you here because our pilots have learnt to finely control those jets and fly in the suits,' said Commander Adams, 'and I think we can help you do the same, Riley.'

'That would be fantastic,' replied Riley.

'Guys, if you'd all follow me,' said Harrison, 'I'll take you to the flight dome.'

They all got up and followed the NASA pilot out of the main building and over to a giant dome shaped hangar. Once inside Harrison took them to a changing area.

'Okay guys, I need you to change into these one-piece flight suits and then come through to the staging area,' said Harrison, pointing towards a door in the corner of the room.

Riley, Casey and Alex took off their clothes, leaving their underwear and socks on and put on the NASA flight suits.

'This is so cool,' said Alex.

'Yeah, you look like a flipping astronaut in that gear,' said Casey. Alex's face beamed with an enormous smile.

'Come on, you two,' said Riley, who was keen to get started.

At the staging area they found Harrison kitting himself up with an antigravity suit.

'Alex, Casey, put these on,' he said pointing to similar suits. 'Riley, can you put on this one. It's similar, has the same protection but without the jets.'

'Yeah of course,' she replied.

They were soon kitted up. Harrison led them down the metal steps and out into the middle of the dome. The space was vast.

'How come this is so big inside?' asked Casey.

'Because it's used to test systems on space craft,' replied Harrison. The girls immediately looked at Alex expecting a geeky comment, but he managed to keep his cool.

Having shown Alex and Casey how to activate and control their suits, Harrison then focussed on Riley.

'Okay,' he said, 'show me what you can do.'

Riley put her arms by her side, focussing her mind, she shot off the ground into the air above them. Harrison followed, slowing to hover in the air next to Riley.

'Very good, Riley,' he said. 'Okay let's go back to your friends on the ground.'

They both lowered themselves slowly back to the ground.

'Okay. Riley, you stay put for a moment while I get these two off the ground,' said Harrison. Alex and Casey followed Harrison's instructions and lifted several metres into the air and lowered back again.

'That was incredible,' exclaimed Alex.

'You've not seen anything yet!' said Harrison.

With that the NASA pilot shot up the roof of the dome then changed direction and flew round its circumference at incredible speed before coming back to join the three teenagers.

'Wow,' said Riley, 'and you think I can do that?'

'With training, yes,' said Harrison.

They spent several more hours developing their flight skills. Harrison showed them how to increase their speed and maintain control. He showed them how to come to a sudden stop mid-air, and much more. Riley, Casey and Alex all found themselves in mid-air about 25 feet from the ground hovering in a circle with Harrison.

'I'm so glad we got to fly with you,' said Casey to Riley.

'Me too,' said Riley.

At the end of the session they removed the suits and got changed.

'We'll do some more tomorrow,' Harrison said, walking them back to the main building.

They spent the night in bunks on site and the following day after breakfast in the site canteen they joined Harrison for further training. Commander Adams came to watch how they were doing during their session. They had mastered a great deal in a very short time. As they came into land, Commander Adams came over to talk to them.

'Good morning,' she said.

'Morning, ma'am,' they replied.

'I had a discussion with Director Andrews this morning and he told me about your training for Secret Service assignments,' she said.

'Yes, ma'am,' replied Riley.

'Well, in light of those future assignments and your progress here, NASA and the Air Force have agreed to loan these flight suits to the Secret Service, exclusively for your use.'

'Wow,' said Alex, 'Thank you, ma'am.'

'Riley, you can also keep the protective flight gear for future use,' added Commander Adams.

'Thank you so much, ma'am,' said Riley.

At the end of their time at NASA, the three of them left with their overnight bags and a special NASA flight pack each. They were taken back to Orlando and put on a flight back to Washington. They dropped the flight packs at Langley for safe keeping on their return. Then, after a busy two days, they headed back to their house in Lee Heights.

Chapter 9

An Unexpected Breakthrough

Back at the house, they found Elsie waiting for them. She cooked them dinner and then left them to relax together. They spent the evening talking about their adventure at NASA and what these suits would mean for their future as a Secret Service Team. Eventually tiredness caught up with them all and they made their way to bed.

The next day, Agent Jacobs arrived after breakfast to take them.

'How come we got a text saying no sports clothes? We doing something different today?' asked Riley.

'No idea,' said Agent Jacobs. 'All I know is the Director of the Secret Service is coming to see you.'

'I wonder what that's about,' said Casey.

Agent Jacobs didn't take the usual route to Langley.

'Where are we heading?' asked Alex.

'FBI Headquarters in DC,' replied Agent Jacobs. When they arrived, they were taken to the office of the FBI Director.

'Morning, sir,' said Riley, Casey and Alex as they walked in.

Luca Jackson was sitting behind his desk and Jack Andrews from the Secret Service was in a chair to the side of the desk.

'I've asked you here this morning because we want the three of you in a DC school for at least the next three days,' said the Director of the Secret Service.

'To do what, sir?' asked Alex.

'You and Casey will go in as Youth Ambassadors,' said Director Jackson. 'Riley, you'll be there too, but you'll be invisible.'

'How come?' asked Riley.

'We've had reports of students getting involved in an

anti-government movement at the school,' said Director Andrews. 'We need you to find out exactly what's going on.'

They were given a full briefing during the morning and after lunch they were taken to the school. When they arrived, Agent Jacobs took them to meet the Principal. Riley was with them, but had already spun herself invisible. As far as the school were concerned, they were only receiving two students for the week.

'Welcome to the Jefferson Memorial High School,' said the Principal. 'I believe you'll be doing some workshops with our younger students as well as being in one of our 11th Grade classes.'

'Yes, sir, we will,' replied Alex and Casey.

'Well, for this afternoon I suggest you both just settle into your new class,' said the Principal.

One of the school administrators took Alex and Casey to a nearby classroom and Riley followed.

'Welcome both of you. Please take a seat,' said the teacher.

'Class, this is Alex and Casey, they're new to the area so I hope you'll make them welcome.'

Alex and Casey looked around the room. Staring back were a lot of unimpressed fifteen and sixteen-year-olds. Alex thought to himself, *I'm so glad I'm not in high school anymore, well not permanently.*

After the registration, the class seemed to split in two. Alex decided to go with one half to Biology and Casey went to Art with the other half.

'This way we are less likely to miss a conversation,' said Alex quietly as everyone was picking bags up and pushing chairs under desks.

Riley came over to them and said she'd meet them in the canteen at break time.

'Where are you going?' whispered Casey.

'I'm going to slip into a few other classes and listen into conversations, see what I can pick up,' she said.

'Be careful,' said Alex. With that the three went their

separate ways.

Riley set off down the corridor. There was the usual crowd of students moving in all directions. *It's just like being back in my high school,* she thought to herself. She followed a group of students heading for the library. Once inside she sat near a group of girls and listened to their conversation. When the bell went sometime later, Riley found the others sat in the canteen with three coffees.

'We thought you'd like a drink,' said Casey.

'Thanks,' said Riley. As she took the cup it disappeared inside her electrical field.

'So, did you two discover anything interesting?' said Alex.

'Not unless hearing how to French kiss a boy counts,' said Riley, laughing.

'Really?' said Casey.

'Yup, it's all those girls talked about for an hour. If I'm honest, it became a little tedious,' replied Riley.

'What about you?' Casey asked Alex.

'Nothing,' he replied.

'I guess for now we try again. Riley has the best chance of finding something as she can move around undetected,' said Casey.

They finished their drinks and left the canteen. As they walked along the corridor, they noticed a large group of boys skulking around near the bathroom. Suddenly, one by one they filed in closing the door behind them.

'What's that all about?' said Casey.

'Let's find out,' said Riley.

The others knew better than to stop her, so the three of them walked towards the bathroom.

'How am I going to get in undetected?' said Riley, looking at the closed door.

'With my help,' said Alex.

He pushed the door open and Riley slipped in. The lads in the bathroom gave him an evil stare, which he knew meant 'go away.'

'Oh, sorry, my bad,' said Alex letting go of the door.

'Great, she's in. Now we wait somewhere nearby for her to come back out,' said Casey.

Much to Riley's surprise there were a couple of girls in the bathroom as well as about six lads. Riley went and stood by the urinals. It seemed to be the only place everyone was staying clear of, and with good reason. Once she'd adjusted herself to the smell of stale wee, she focussed on what was happening in front of her.

'Listen to me,' said one of the boys, 'you just don't get it, do you?'

'I do,' said another boy, 'our government is wrecking our futures. But how does a secret meeting in a school toilet solve that?'

'It doesn't, you idiot,' said one of the girls. 'If you want in, you'll have to meet us after school.'

'I want in,' said the second boy to speak.

Riley noticed that none of them had said names. She thought quickly to herself. Remembering back to the cafe and the gang who'd planned the assassination of the President, she took out her phone. Making sure it was still on silent and the flash was disabled, she moved around the group slowly taking pictures of all their faces. Moments after she finished the bell rang for lessons. The students in the bathroom started to leave. Riley took the opportunity to follow the largest group of them to see which class they were in. Alex and Casey watched as she headed down the corridor. Realising she was still undercover, they decided to let her go and meet up later.

Riley followed four of the boys and one girl into a classroom. There were lots of other students there. Riley stood at the front with the teacher so she could see where the students sat. As the teacher called the register, Riley made a mental note of the names: Wendy, Ted, Rex, Danny and Adam. She wandered round the class and noticed that all of the books had 11R next to the name. *Brilliant,* she thought to herself. *I've got the names of five of the eight and the form they're in. Good start.* None of them said anything more during that lesson.

At the end of the day, Alex and Casey found Riley on the front path of the school.

'Hey you, what's been going on?' said Alex,

'I'll tell you later,' said Riley, 'but for now I need you to go with Agent Jacobs and follow me at a distance. I'm going with this group as they're taking their friend to some anti-government meeting.'

'Okay,' said Alex.

'Stay safe,' said Casey as the two of them made their way across the road to Agent Jacobs and the 4x4.

Alex explained to Agent Jacobs what was going on and he radioed it in.

'Okay,' he said, 'we've got clearance to conduct surveillance.'

Riley walked along with the students she'd photographed in the boys' bathroom. They didn't say much. She guessed that they didn't want to be overheard by other students on the sidewalk. After several blocks, the group turned down a narrow side street. Agent Jacobs pulled the 4x4 up on the far side of the junction and watched as Riley walked down the side road with the group. They stopped outside a bookstore.

'In here,' said one of them.

'Once you go in, you're committed to this,' said one of the girls.

'I know,' said the boy they'd questioned in the bathroom.

'Okay, inside,' said another boy, pointing through the open door. The group disappeared out of sight into the store.

'What now?' said Casey.

'We wait,' said Agent Jacobs.

Inside Riley followed them to the basement of the store. There she found several other students from different schools and a few adults. She decided that best thing she could do would be to listen and gather as much intelligence as possible. She stood in the corner of the room where she had a view of everyone. Taking out her phone, she switched the camera on to film. Over the following hour, she captured the faces of every person in the room and some radical anti-establishment political views from a number of them. What piqued her interest was a closing comment from one of the adults leading the meeting.

'Next time we meet,' he said, 'I'll be sharing our plans with you. Time for talk is over, the time for action has come!'

There was an almost audible cheer from the group, clearly motivated to take their beliefs to the next level.

Riley made her way back upstairs with the intelligence she'd gathered. She felt a sense of relief when she was out of the bookstore. She noticed the 4x4 at the end of the street and headed for it. Before getting inside she made herself visible.

'We need to see Director Jackson,' she said.

'Very well,' said Agent Jacobs as he turned the car around to head towards FBI H.Q.

On the way he radioed in that Riley was safe and they were coming to see the Director.

Sitting down with Director Jackson, Riley explained the events of the day and showed them the photographs and film on her phone.

'This is great intelligence work,' said Luca, 'especially as you had to do it on instinct. Next time we can prepare a little better and have more back up available.'

'Thank you, sir,' said Riley.

'So, what's next, sir?' asked Alex.

'I need you to be at that meeting,' said Luca. 'We need to know what they're planning.'

'I can do that, sir,' said Riley.

'Very well. Go home, get some rest and Agent Jacobs will take you back to the high school in the morning. We can let this play out and see where it goes.'

That evening the three of them sat in the lounge in the house in Lee Heights.

'Wow,' said Casey, 'you're a proper Secret Service Agent now.'

'We all are,' replied Riley.

'Yeah but it's you doing this with your abilities,' said Casey.

'None of which I'd know how to use or be confident to use without you both there to back me up. We're a team. We always will be,' said Riley.

Elsie made them dinner before heading home.

'Don't be up too late, you three,' she said on her way out of the door.

Chapter 10

The Bookstore Plot

They arrived at school early the next morning and went to the canteen for a drink. Riley had spun invisible in the house before they set off. This had thrown Agent Jacobs as he didn't know if she was in the car or not.

'She's definitely here?' he asked Casey.

'Right next to you,' came her reply. Agent Jacobs looked at the empty seat.

'Okay,' he said, as he set off for the Jefferson Memorial High School.

Drinking their coffees in the canteen, the three of them discussed the plan for the day.

'Casey and I will try and find out the names of the three students not in 11R,' said Alex.

'And I'll stay close to the others and see if anything develops during the day,' said Riley.

'Okay, take care, won't you?' said Casey.

'Always,' replied Riley, before getting up and leaving the others.

'Sometimes I wish we still had our invisibility so she didn't have to do this alone,' said Casey.

'She's not alone, she has us, but I know what you mean,' said Alex.

Later in the day Riley followed her 11R group to the school library. The five students she was watching had separated themselves from the rest of the class and were now sitting around one of the computers.

'Have you got it?' said one of the boys.

'Yeah, relax, will you?' said another as he took a pen drive from his pocket and plugged it into the computer.

Riley moved to get a better view of the computer screen.

'So, what does this thing do?' asked the girl in the group.

'It overrides the school's internet security and gets us

direct access to the dark web,' came the reply.

They all watched as a computer programme seemed to be running with various numbers and codes moving up the screen. Suddenly the screen went black, then a symbol Riley had never seen before appeared. She quickly got out her phone and photographed it before it vanished.

'Here we go,' said one of the boys, as images of terrorist attacks and weapons appeared on screen.

'Is this what we'll be doing?' asked one of the boys.

'I guess we'll find out at the meeting tonight. Don't forget to be at the bookstore for 9.00 p.m.'

Riley decided she had all the information she needed for now so left the library in search of Alex and Casey. She found them in the gym. Their class was having a games lesson and they'd not found a way to escape it. Riley sat and watched as Alex and Casey scaled the ropes with ease. All those weeks of training with Koba had definitely paid off. Finally, the lesson finished and they came over to speak to her.

'Everything okay?' asked Casey.

'Yeah, I'll tell you what I've discovered once you're changed,' replied Riley.

Alex and Casey went off to their respective changing rooms and got out of their gym clothes. Once they were dressed, they found Riley in the corridor.

'Go on then,' said Alex, 'tell us what's been happening.'

Riley explained about the dark web, the strange symbol and the time and place for the next meeting.

'We will need to be at that,' said Alex.

'Yeah, we are going to have to speak to the FBI as soon as school ends,' said Riley.

'Tell us about this symbol,' said Casey.

'I can do better than that,' said Riley, taking her phone out to show them the photograph. They looked at the image of half a skull with an axe embedded in the side.

'I wonder what it stands for?' said Casey.

'I guess I'll find out later,' said Riley.

'Whatever it is, it doesn't look good,' said Alex.

Alex and Casey hadn't had any luck getting the names of the other students so they spent the rest of the afternoon trying. Riley met them on the school path at the end of the day. Agent Jacobs was waiting for them.

'Is Riley in the car?' he asked.

'Yeah she's here,' replied Alex.

'We need to go to FBI H.Q.,' said Casey.

'Okay,' said Agent Jacobs, 'has there been a development?'

'Yes, Riley has gathered more intel on the group,' said Alex.

Soon they arrived at the J. Edgar Hoover Building on Pennsylvania Avenue. As they got out of the car, they could see agents coming and going from the building's main entrance. Once inside they made their way to Director Jackson's office.

'Thank you for seeing us, Director,' said Alex.

'Is it just the two of you today?' he said.

'Oh no sir, Riley is here,' Alex said.

Casey looked at Riley, she was still invisible to everyone except her and Alex.

'Need a hand?' said Casey.

'Yes, please,' said Riley, standing up.

Riley span herself round and round until the brain burn started. When she reappeared she was in Casey's arms. Casey had stopped her from falling as the burn in her head sometimes hurt, making her lose balance.

'That never gets old,' said Luca. 'Now, what do you have for me?'

Riley and Casey sat down. Riley explained what she'd seen and heard in the library. She showed the Director the image of the skull and axe and told him about the 9.00 p.m. meeting.

'We've seen this image before. It's a white supremacy hate group called the First World Order. We didn't know they were recruiting teenagers from local schools, though. We have to get you to this meeting tonight,' said the Director.

'What do you need from us?' said Casey.

'Right now, I need you to go to our canteen and have a meal. It'll take me a while to put a team together for an operation that's only five hours away. I'll see you in the briefing room at 7.00 p.m.,' he replied.

'Yes, sir,' said Alex, as they all got up to leave.

Sitting in the canteen at the FBI H.Q. felt a little surreal. They had to keep reminding themselves they were Special Agents now as they still just felt like friends on a wild adventure.

'I wonder what Director Jackson is putting in place for this operation,' said Casey.

'I expect it's what we've been taught about in our training. Communications, backup personnel, specialist equipment in case weapons are involved,' said Alex.

'Stop, you're scaring me now,' said Riley.

'Hey,' said Casey putting her arm round Riley, 'you'll be fine. Remember you've been in there before. Just stay out of the way and make observations. You're not there to stop anything.'

'Casey's right,' said Alex, 'you've had a lot of training now so you're better equipped for this. Certainly, more so than when we stopped the assassination of the President.'

'That feels like a lifetime ago,' said Riley.

'Excuse me,' said a female agent. 'The Director is ready to brief you now.'

They got up and followed her through the building to a large briefing room. In the room were six other FBI agents and Agent Jacobs from the Secret Service.

'Okay everyone, let's get started,' said Director Jackson. 'Based on intel gathered from an ongoing undercover operation we are running jointly with the Secret Service we have learnt about a meeting in DC this evening. Riley, please can you share what you know?'

Riley, was slightly taken aback by the request. She pointed at herself. The Director nodded and she got up looking tentatively at Alex and Casey as she walked to the front.

She hated standing in front of kids in school but this was different and somehow, she found her confidence. Speaking clearly and boldly she explained what she knew about the First World Order and what they had been doing in the Jefferson Memorial High School.

'Thanks,' said Luca, as she sat back down.

'Well done,' said Casey quietly, patting her on the shoulder.

'Okay, so the plan is for Riley to go back into the bookstore this evening and listen in to the cell's plans. We are there purely as a backup. I don't want to engage the cell at this stage, just collect more intelligence on their operation. Is that clear?'

'Yes, sir,' came a joint reply for everyone in the room.

'Very well, please make your way to the armoury and I'll see you outside shortly.'

Riley, Casey and Alex followed the other agents to the armoury where they were each given a bulletproof vest.

'Haven't worn one of these for a while!' said Riley.

Casey was struggling to fit hers correctly so Riley gave her some help. They were all given radio headsets to communicate. Once they'd finished kitting up, they went to join the Director in the command vehicle going to the bookstore.

They parked a block away. Riley climbed into the back of the vehicle which was a large van with computer systems in it. She spun around to become invisible again before heading off towards the bookstore. When she arrived, all was quiet.

'Alex, do you read me?' she said.

'I read you,' he replied. 'What's the situation?'

'It's all quiet, no-one around,' she replied. Alex relayed this to the Director.

'Tell her to stay put and wait,' said Luca. He was relaying messages through Alex because the electrical field that hid Riley meant only Alex and Casey could see and hear her when she was invisible. This seemed to work over the radio too, although no-one had quite figured out why.

Alex relayed the command and Riley stepped back into the shadows near the bookstore and waited. Suddenly a small group of teenagers appeared on the corner of the street.

'They're here,' said Riley.

'We can see them from our position,' replied Alex. As the group arrived, they walked right past Riley and opened the bookstore door.

'I'm going in,' said Riley, as she slipped through the doorway behind the last teenager.

She followed the group down to the basement where she found the same adults from the previous day waiting for them. There was someone new there this time. Looking at him sent a shiver down Riley's spine. The man was white, in his late thirties and bald. He had an eye patch on his right eye and a horrific scar that ran out from the eye patch onto his cheek and forehead. *I dread to think what's under that eye patch,* thought Riley.

Everyone sat down and one of the adults spoke.

'Thanks for coming,' he said, 'it shows your loyalty to our cause and the future of our nation,' he added. 'I want to introduce you to Chris Cannons; you will address him as Commander.'

Riley, realising this was the top dog, took out her phone to record what the Commander was about to share. Everyone was silent, all eyes fixed on their leader.

'You are the privileged few,' he said, 'the best this world has to offer. After tonight you'll be its hope for the future.'

The teenagers looked at each other, smiling.

The Commander continued, 'Tonight we will prepare a huge global attack that will eliminate the corruption in two major governments in this failing world of ours.'

Riley couldn't believe what she was hearing. Her heart was pounding so hard she was convinced the Commander would hear the drumming in her chest. She breathed and focussed.

'You will all take part in an operation to destroy the US Capitol,' said the Commander. 'At the same time our allies in London will destroy their parliament on the same day.'

He stepped back and the other man stepped forward to speak again.

'In order to maintain our cover, we will be letting life go on as normal. No-one will expect a group of high school kids. However, this means you leave here with the knowledge to thwart our plans. Understand this, anyone who is found to be talking to the wrong person about this will be executed.'

Riley was convinced her heart had stopped beating. One of the teenagers stood up.

'You have our loyalty, sir,' she said. The others stood and they all saluted the Commander.

'Very well,' said the Commander, stepping forward again. 'We will meet tomorrow to go through the operation which will take place in ten days.'

'Sir, isn't that the 4th July?' said the girl who'd stood up first.

'It is,' said the Commander. 'It'll become the day the world found its independence from the corruption that has crippled it for far too long.'

They saluted again and then filed out.

'9.00 p.m. tomorrow,' said one of the adults, as the teenagers, with Riley in tow, climbed the stairs from the basement and made their way through the bookstore.

Chapter 11

The Scare

The teenagers quickly dispersed on the street outside the bookstore. Riley made her way back to the FBI Command Vehicle. Once inside she spun visible again and showed the Director what she'd discovered.

'Good Lord,' said the Director, 'we've been after Cannons for years. Never been this close before. Well done, Riley. This phone footage is superb evidence against him.'

'Thank you, sir,' said Riley.

'Okay,' said Director Jackson, 'I'm going to ask Jacobs to take you three home for now. Elsie has stayed late to give you some supper. I want you in school tomorrow as normal and then come to H.Q. straight after. Basically, we will repeat today and see what other intel we can gather. Then we need to plan a response ready for the 4th July.'

The three of them changed vehicles and as the rest of the team headed back to H.Q., they crossed the river and headed home.

'Late finish today,' said Elsie, as they came into the kitchen. They weren't too sure whether she was talking about them or herself.

'Yeah, looks like it'll be a late one tomorrow too!' said Alex.

Elsie handed them all a bowl of home-made chicken soup and some crusty bread.

'Thanks, Elsie,' said Casey.

They ate their food and went through to the lounge.

After Elsie had gone, Alex and Casey asked Riley what it had been like to be in the room with this international terrorist.

'To be honest, I thought I was going to have a heart attack. I could feel my heart pounding in my chest. But somehow, I got control and focused on my mission. I'm just glad we have usable intel. I hope we get everything we need tomorrow,' she said.

'So do I,' said Casey. 'I don't like it that you have to go in there alone.'

'Well, hopefully the FBI will be able to take over after tomorrow,' said Riley.

They decided that bed was the best plan as another long day lay ahead of them. Riley went to her room and put her pyjama shorts and vest on while Casey was in the bathroom. Casey came out of the bathroom wearing similar nightwear. Riley noticed Casey's lightning scar on her thigh.

'That's completely healed now, hasn't it?' said Riley.

'Yeah, has yours?' asked Casey.

Riley lifted her shorts a little higher on her leg so Casey could see the entire scar.

'Yeah, seems to,' she replied, letting the fabric of her shorts drop back into place.

'Does yours hurt anymore?' asked Riley.

'Only occasionally,' said Casey, 'it does feel strange though.'

'In what way?' asked Riley.

'Feel,' said Casey. Riley put her hand on Casey's thigh and ran it over the scar.

'You're right, that does feel strange,' said Riley. 'It's hot.'

'Isn't yours like that?' said Casey.

'No, it just feels like the rest of my leg,' said Riley.

Casey put her hand on Riley's thigh and ran her fingers over her scar.

Taking her hand away she said, 'That's weird. I wonder why mine is hot and yours isn't.'

'I wonder if Alex's scar is like yours,' said Riley.

'Well he's gone to bed so we'll have to ask him tomorrow,' said Casey.

'Talking of bed, I should get to mine,' said Riley.

'Yeah, me too,' said Casey.

They said goodnight and Riley went to use the bathroom before turning in for the night.

THE SCARE

The morning came all too quickly. Riley got up as soon as her alarm went off and made her way to the bathroom for a shower. She was first downstairs so put the kettle on for coffee. Elsie was already there as always preparing breakfast for the three of them. They'd never have got through the last month without her help. Casey and Alex arrived in the kitchen together.

'Hot like mine,' said Casey sitting down at the table.

'Excuse me?' said Riley in an enquiring tone.

'His scar,' added Casey, pointing at Alex's leg.

'Oh,' said Riley.

'No idea, how this became a topic of conversation,' said Alex, 'but it's strange yours isn't hot and ours are.'

'Maybe your lightning energy is in the scar and mine is still in my brain,' said Riley.

'It's the best theory we have,' said Casey.

'Yeah and we will have to leave it at that as we have more pressing concerns,' said Alex.

'Are you two ready for today?' he asked.

'Yeah, as ready as we can be,' replied Riley.

It wasn't long before Agent Jacobs arrived to take them to school. They had got used to him being part of their day. As usual, he asked if Riley was in the car.

'I don't know why you ask every day,' said Casey. 'Surely you see your passenger door open and close by itself!' He smiled as if to say, 'of course I do,' but said nothing and set off for school instead.

The rest of the school day was much the same as the day before except Casey managed to get the names of the remaining gang members by attending a Chemistry lesson they were in.

'Great job,' said Alex.

'Thanks,' said Casey as they walked back to meet Agent Jacobs at the end of the day.

On arrival at the FBI Headquarters they were told to go and have something to eat. Then, as the day before, they were collected from the canteen and taken to a briefing room where Director Jackson was waiting to address the team. As they walked in, they noticed the Director of the Secret Service was also in the room.

'I've asked Director Andrews to join us as this is a multi-agency operation,' said Luca.

Luca continued going through the plan for the operation which was very similar to the day before.

'The main thing is that Riley gets in and out again safely and undetected,' said Luca.

After the briefing they went to the armoury to collect their communications equipment and body armour.

It wasn't long before Riley was standing alone outside the bookstore waiting to see if the teenagers from her school would appear.

She radioed in, 'They're on their way down the street.'

'Roger that,' replied Alex.

Once again, she followed the group down to the basement. Just as the previous night there were other teenagers and adults there, also, Chris Cannons, one of the FBI's most wanted men. Riley went and stood in the same corner as the night before next to a side cabinet which had old books stacked on its top.

'Okay, sit down and be quiet, as quick as you can,' said the same man from the night before.

Apart from their leader, no-one had given their names, but thanks to Riley's photographs, a number of the suspects had been matched on the FBI and NSA databases. Chris Cannons stood up.

'Right,' he said, 'let's get straight to the point. Nine days from now we will bring down the US and UK governments. Each of you will be entering the Capitol as part of a school trip. The leadership here will be your teachers. Everyone in the group will carry an element of a major explosive device. Each part on its own will appear to be harmless and of no consequence to security. However, combined, these elements will turn these corrupt institutions to dust!' said the Commander. 'We will meet here again the night before the attack.' With that he sat back down.

Riley had been filming when all of a sudden, her phone

slipped out of her hand. The thud it made on the floor made everyone look her way.

Jumping to his feet, Cannons said, 'What the hell was that?'

Taking out his gun he walked towards Riley. Thinking quickly and with her heart pounding, Riley bent down, grabbed her phone. She then crawled under the side cabinet. She watched, terrified, as Cannons waved his gun around where she'd been standing moments before.

'There's nothing there, sir,' said one of the teenagers.

'What was that bang, then?' replied Cannons.

'It's an old building, sir,' said one of the adults.

'Maybe,' said Cannons.

Riley, who hadn't taken a breath since he walked over, breathed a sigh of relief when Cannons finally turned around and went back to his seat. She slowly and very quietly got out from under the cabinet.

'Right, you lot,' said one of the adults, 'off you go and remember, keep your mouths shut or we will kill you.'

'Yes, sir!' they all replied together, saluting the Commander.

Riley followed them out before the door closed. She was so relieved to be out of the bookstore that she ran down the road to the FBI command vehicle waiting a block away.

Once inside she spun visible and collapsed into a chair.

'You okay?' asked Casey. 'What happened?'

Riley was shaking. Casey knelt on the floor of the van and took hold of her hands.

'Hey, you're safe now,' she said. Riley looked at her, then at Alex and Luca.

'Sorry, that really shook me up,' she said.

'What happened?' asked the FBI Director.

'I dropped my phone while filming Cannons. It must have landed outside my electrical field as they heard the bang on the floor. I managed to pick it up and move under a side cabinet before Cannons came over with his gun. It was all too close for comfort,' said Riley.

'Okay, well it's over now,' said Luca, 'let's go back to

Headquarters and debrief.'

They headed back and met with Director Andrews to update him on the terror threat.

'Okay, I want the three of you to meet with the President in the White House tomorrow morning,' said Director Andrews. 'Luca, can you attend the meeting too?'

'Of course,' replied Director Jackson.

'Very well,' said Director Andrews, 'let's get these three home.'

When Agent Jacobs dropped them off, they went into their house to find Elsie warming soup up for them. They all went and got into their pyjamas and came back down for the soup.

'You three look shattered,' said Elsie.

'We are,' said Alex. 'It's been a very stressful day.'

'Well, have your supper and go straight to bed,' said Elsie. 'The rest will do you good.'

'Thank you, Elsie,' said Casey.

Riley was very quiet through supper. After they'd cleared away, they all went upstairs. Alex said goodnight and left the girls on the landing. Casey was about to say goodnight when Riley interrupted.

'I don't want to be alone,' she said.

'Do you want me to stay with you?' asked Casey.

'Would you mind?' said Riley, shaking again.

She was clearly still in shock from the events of that evening.

'Not at all,' said Casey taking her hand and leading her into the bedroom. The girls climbed into bed together and Casey switched off the light. She lay on her side behind Riley and put her arm round her. Riley sighed and stopped shaking.

'Get some sleep,' said Casey.

'I'll try,' replied Riley as she took hold of Casey's hand and closed her eyes.

Chapter 12

Operation Legion

Casey woke the next day to find Riley still holding her hand.

'Hey you,' she said, 'time to wake up.'

'What?' said Riley in a drowsy muffled voice.

'Time to get up,' repeated Casey.

Riley turned over to face her friend. 'Hey,' she said.

'Did you sleep okay?' said Casey.

'Yeah, I did. Thanks for staying with me,' said Riley.

'Anytime, and yeah I know you're not gay like me but I'm here for you as a friend anytime you need this,' said Casey.

Riley gave Casey a big hug.

'Thank you,' she said, 'now we'd better get up.'

The girls appeared at breakfast together some time later.

'Morning,' said Alex.

'Morning,' they replied as they sat down for breakfast.

'How are you feeling this morning, Riley?' asked Alex.

'Much better, thanks,' said Riley.

After they'd had their breakfast, they set off with Agent Jacobs for the White House. On arrival they showed their Secret Service badges to the security guard on the gate. Once inside the West Wing, they met with Grace the White House Chief of Staff. She took them through to the Oval Office.

'Riley, Casey, Alex come in,' said the President.

'Thank you, sir,' said Riley.

Sitting down they looked around to see who else was there. The Directors of the FBI, CIA, NSA and Secret Service, plus the President's National Security Advisor were there, all of whom they'd met before. Also, in the room was someone they'd not met before.

'Can I introduce you to Agent Martin Shepherd,' said the President. 'He works for MI5.' They all said hello.

'We thought it prudent to involve British Intelligence based on your discovery this week,' said Director Andrews.

Riley sat forward on the sofa and looked straight at the President.

'So, what's the plan, sir?'

'I'll let Director Andrews explain,' replied the President. Jack stood up so he could see everyone clearly.

'Based on intel gathered by Riley's team we now know that in eight days both Washington and London face a major terror threat. As a result, we are launching "Operation Legion" so called because of its many elements. The operation will involve security and intelligence services on both sides of the pond. We have enough leads to follow all the members of the Washington cell. So, the FBI and Secret Service will deal with the threat here. We want Riley, Casey and Alex to go to London with James from the CIA. He will act as your liaison with MI5. Your role there is to gather intelligence on the London cell and help their Security Service prevent the attack on the Houses of Parliament.'

There was a pause as everyone took in the details of Director Andrews briefing.

Then Alex spoke. 'But we don't know where the London cell is operating from,' he said.

Martin spoke up. 'Actually, we think we do. Since the FBI shared its intel with us, we've discovered a school in South London which has shown an unusual number of pupils accessing the dark web. We believe the First World Order may be radicalising them. We'd like to place you and Casey as exchange students, and Riley undercover, in the school,' he said.

'Of course, anything we can do,' said Riley.

'Okay, everyone, I'll let you go and prepare. Please keep me informed of developments,' said the President. Various agency directors responded with 'Yes sir' as everyone got up to leave. Riley, Casey and Alex went with Director Andrews.

'I'm going to arrange for you to go home to Lee Heights. You'll have an hour before Agent Jacobs takes you to

Langley,' said Jack. 'Once you arrive, Martin, James and the three of you will have a briefing with Director Montgomery. You'll then go to Dulles International Airport where a plane will take you to London Heathrow,' said Director Andrews.

Back in Lee Heights, Riley put a bag on her bed and opened her wardrobe up.

'So, what does a Secret Service agent on an international mission pack for the weekend?' she said out loud.

'We heard that!' said Casey laughing.

Riley blushed and started to laugh as well. A short while later the three of them were putting bags in the hallway ready to go. They went through to the kitchen and Alex made them all a coffee. Opening a packet of Oreos, they sat at the kitchen table to have their drinks.

'I can't believe we are going to London,' said Casey.

'Yeah and working with MI5,' said Riley.

'I just hope we can find this terror cell and stop them,' said Alex.

A car horn honked outside the house. Riley opened the door to see James from the CIA parking up. He and Martin got out and opened the trunk.

'You three ready to go?' asked James.

'Yeah, we're ready,' said Riley picking up her bag.

The others followed her to the car. As they placed their bags in the trunk, they noticed three NASA flight packs.

'Great,' said Alex, 'did Director Montgomery give you those?'

'Yes,' replied James, 'what are they?'

'Anti-gravity suits,' said Alex.

'We've been trained to fly them,' added Casey.

Riley looked at her two friends then at James and said, 'I can fly without one!'

'Of course you can!' replied James, smiling.

Casey rolled her eyes and gently pushed Riley saying, 'Get in the car, show off!'

As they set off, Riley asked, 'What happened to us going to a briefing with Director Montgomery?'

'Change of plan,' said James, 'the Director is dealing with a major incident that's just flared up in the Middle East. So, he's given me mission details to share with you.'

'Ah, okay,' said Riley.

It wasn't long before they were checking into Dulles Airport. The flight to London would take a little over seven hours. Riley wasn't very good at sleeping on planes. She'd not had a great deal of experience flying but when she had she'd never slept. She was glad to find her seat had its own television screen. As the plane took off, she sat scrolling through the movie listings to see if there was anything worth watching. Alex and Casey were sitting either side of Riley. Alex had the window and Casey the aisle seat. It wasn't long before they'd both dozed off, leaving Riley with the airline movie collection for company. Fortunately, she found a film to watch which helped a couple of hours pass by.

Once the flight arrived at Heathrow, the five of them collected baggage and set off for MI5 H.Q. at Thames House. Although they were all tired from the journey, Martin's boss was keen to meet Riley and her team. He also wanted to set things in motion as there was now only a week left to stop the attack!

'Welcome to the UK, my name is Sir Richard Marsden and I'm the Director General of Her Majesty's Security Service, which you call MI5.'

'Thank you,' replied Riley. 'I'm Special Agent Riley Bennett, this is Casey Johnson and Alex Manning from the US Secret Service.'

'Well, now the introductions are over, if you'd follow me please,' said Sir Richard. He led them to a large office with a conference table.

'Take a seat, everyone,' he said.

Once seated, Sir Richard introduced them to more MI5 officers and started to explain what was happening at the British end of Operation Legion. He told them about the high school which had been identified as a possible recruiting site for the First World Order.

'I believe you want Casey and I in there as exchange

students,' said Alex.

'Correct,' said Sir Richard, 'and Riley will be there undercover. Although I'm not entirely sure how that will work,' he added.

'Would you like me to show you?' asked Riley.

'If you don't mind,' said Sir Richard.

Riley stood up and found some space.

'What I'm about to show you is highly classified and must only be discussed those who need to know,' she said, before signalling to Alex to be ready to catch her.

Riley started to spin round and round until her body speed matched the electrical energy from the lightning that was going around her brain. Then suddenly the brain burn started and she vanished from view. As she went, Alex grabbed her to stop her falling.

'Incredible,' said Sir Richard, 'and can you still see her?'

'Yes, sir,' said Alex.

'So where is she now?'

'Behind you, sir,' said Alex as Sir Richard turned to see a painting on the wall moving on its own.

Once Riley had reappeared and returned to her seat, the Director General continued.

'We need Riley's team to find out how many members are in the cell, where they're based and what they plan to do. We suspect it's something similar to the US cell as they're using high school kids to carry it out.'

'No offence, sir, but aren't we also making use of high school kids, putting Riley and co into this situation?' said one of the officers present.

'We are, but these three have CIA training for this. The kids being recruited by the FWO do not,' replied Sir Richard.

'When do we start?' asked Riley.

'Tomorrow morning,' said Sir Richard. 'We've arranged for you three and James to stay in a local hotel. Martin will collect you in the morning and take you to the school.'

'Very well, sir,' said Alex.

With that they left Thames House and were taken to a

nearby hotel. It was getting close to midnight London time and even though they didn't feel overtired they all decided to get to bed. After all, tomorrow was a new day and a new school in a new country.

The next day Riley woke early. Getting out of bed she went through to her en-suite bathroom to take a shower. The long flight had left her feeling sweaty and she was glad to freshen up. She was also grateful the hotel's hair dryer was really powerful as she'd forgotten to pack an adapter plug for hers. She joined the others downstairs for breakfast. Alex was filling up on bacon, eggs and sausages.

'Don't overdo it,' said Casey, 'you need to be able to stay on your game all day and not dose off on a full belly.'

'Yes, Mom!' replied Alex smiling.

After breakfast Agent Martin Shepherd arrived to take Alex and Casey to school. Riley had made herself invisible in her room after breakfast and was ready to join her friends in the car.

'I'll see you all later,' said James, who was heading back to Thames House to act as the CIA Liaison.

Riley, Casey and Alex got in the car to go. The journey took about thirty minutes, not because of the distance, but just the level of traffic in the capital.

Chapter 13

Back to School

Martin didn't come in with them. He gave them directions to the main office and told them to ask for the Head, whose name was Miss Carr. They had no trouble finding her and she was very welcoming.

'Follow me, please,' she said, as she led Alex and Casey to a year 11 class. Riley quietly tagged along behind, keeping her presence hidden from Miss Carr.

Alex and Casey were introduced and found seats. Riley did her usual thing of standing near the front to start getting a good look at the pupils. She quickly noticed a girl who didn't seem to be paying attention to the teacher but had a crowd of others focussed on her antics. This girl reminded Riley of Christine from her actual school back home. Well, Christine before she was free of her horrible dad and still being a mean girl in school. Riley watched as this girl continued to disrupt the lesson. As the lesson drew to an end Riley told Alex she was going to follow the girl she'd been watching. Alex and Casey agreed to keep their distance but back her up.

Out in the corridor Riley followed the girl as she met up with two boys from another class before heading out onto the school yard. The three of them headed towards some bike sheds. A few pupils rode bikes to school and would leave them locked in the sheds during the day. No-one generally went near them which made it the perfect place for a private conversation.

As Riley got closer, she saw another girl was already there waiting for them.

'You took your time, Karen!' said the waiting girl.

'Yeah sorry, Amy, the lesson overran coz some exchange kids showed up,' said Karen, the girl Riley had followed.

'Did they give you the details?'

'Yeah, but it's only for friends, right. Please don't go bringing strangers along,' said Amy. Amy handed Karen a piece of paper.

'It's all on there. Time, place and so on,' she said.

'Thanks,' replied Karen as she and the two lads with her walked off.

Riley decided to find Alex and Casey. It wasn't difficult as they had kept their distance and were across the school yard waiting for her.

'So, what were they talking about?' said Alex.

'Some meeting but it's all written down on a piece of paper which Karen now has in her bag.'

'Who's Karen?' asked Casey.

'The girl I followed from your lesson,' replied Riley.

'We need to know what's on that paper,' said Alex.

'And how are we gonna do that?' said Casey.

'I'll sort it,' said Riley.

The next lesson they had was a lab-based Chemistry lesson. Everyone was so focussed on their experiments it was easy to sit on the floor right next to Karen's bag and rifle through it unnoticed. After the lesson Alex and Casey asked Riley what she'd seen.

'Just an address and time,' she replied. 'Saturday 8.00 p.m., at an address in a place called Sanderstead.'

'That's tomorrow,' said Alex.

'We will have to go along and see,' said Casey.

'We'd better inform MI5,' said Alex. 'We can't go to an unknown address without proper back up.'

Riley continued to watch Karen that afternoon, but nothing stuck out as unusual or suspicious. Well no more than a typical teen wanting all the attention in school, that is! At the end of the day the three of them crossed the road outside school and got into the car. Martin and James were both inside waiting for them.

'How was your first day?' said Martin.

'Okay, thanks,' said Casey.

'We think we may have a tenuous lead,' said Alex.

'Why tenuous?' asked James.

'Because it's nothing definite,' replied Casey. 'Just a hunch.'

'A lot of good police work is done on just a hunch,' said Martin. 'So, what have you got?'

'There's a get-together tomorrow, 8.00 p.m., at this address in Sanderstead,' said Alex showing Martin a slip of paper with the details on.

'Okay, posh neighbourhood that one. Well we can get a team mobilised to cover you and we can see what's there,' said Martin.

Martin drove them back to their hotel. Riley made herself visible again in her room, falling onto her bed with the brain burn. The three of them joined James for dinner in the hotel restaurant that evening.

'Martin is going to pick us up at 12.00 p.m. tomorrow to go to Thames House so you can get a bit of a rest beforehand,' he said.

'Great,' said Casey, 'I'm still tired from the flight here!' After dinner they returned to their rooms. Riley didn't feel as tired as Casey, which was strange as she'd been the one who couldn't sleep on the plane. She put on her pyjamas and decided to get out her sketchbook. Sitting on her bed she started sketching a portrait of Alex.

I'll surprise him with it once it's finished, she thought to herself.

The next day Riley woke to hear knocking on her door.

'Hang on,' she said clambering out of bed. She walked over to the door and looked through the spy hole. Opening the door, she saw Casey standing there.

'Do you mind if I use your en-suite?' asked Casey. 'My shower is broken.'

'No, of course not. Come in,' replied Riley.

'Thanks,' said Casey. 'Sorry if I woke you.'

'Don't worry. I would have been getting up soon anyway as I need to wash my hair,' replied Riley.

They took it in turns to have a shower. They then sat together in the hotel's bath robes and did each other's hair.

Riley was so pleased to have a friend to do this with. After so long hiding from people at school, it was great to have a best friend.

'I need to get dressed,' said Casey.

'Okay,' said Riley, 'I'll call for you and Alex in a bit and we can go to breakfast together.'

With that, Casey got up and headed back to her room.

At breakfast they discussed what this meeting in Sanderstead might be.

'It could be similar to the bookstore,' said Riley, sounding a little anxious.

'Or it could be something completely different,' said Alex. 'So there is no point in getting worried about it.'

'Alex is right,' said Casey, 'let's wait and see what MI5 say and take it from there, eh?'

'Good idea,' said Riley taking some more toast from the rack.

James joined them quite late and grabbed some breakfast before the buffet shut.

'Oversleep, did we?' said Casey.

'Just a bit,' he replied. 'I don't often get a lie in with this job.'

By the time he'd finished, Martin had arrived to take them to Thames House.

As they arrived at Thames House, they were joined by several MI5 officers. Everyone made their way to the briefing room. Once seated, Martin introduced Section Chief Katy Roberts.

'Good afternoon everyone,' she said. 'We are preparing for an intelligence gathering op as part of Operation Legion with our partners from the American Secret Service,' she gestured towards Riley and friends.

'Based on intel gather from a London high school we've had surveillance on, we are going to an address in Sanderstead, South London. We believe a meeting to be taking place around 8.00 p.m. tonight.'

'What is the nature of the meeting?' asked one of the officers.

'That we don't know,' said the Section Chief. 'As a result, the plan is to send Riley in undercover. Depending on the nature of the meeting, we will provide direct backup on site or keep our distance.'

'Is that wise?' said one of the officers looking at Riley. He was clearly judging her based on appearance.

Riley looked at him and raised her eyebrows, but said nothing, leaving it for Katy to respond.

'Absolutely,' said the Section Chief. 'Riley is US Secret Service, with CIA training. She also has some highly classified abilities to use for this kind of operation.'

Riley smiled a little, not making it too obvious she was pleased the officer had been put in his place.

After further details of the operation were discussed, they took a break. Everyone was ordered to meet at the armoury at 5.00 p.m. to be kitted out for the operation and then make the journey out of the city to Sanderstead. When Riley arrived at the armoury with Casey and Alex, they found body amour had been put out for them. They were used to this at the FBI armoury. They had no trouble getting into the bullet proof vests and connecting up the communications equipment, much to the surprise of the MI5 officers around them.

Martin came in and told them the Section Chief had given him operational command and that Riley's team would travel with him in the command vehicle. The convoy of three vehicles, with a total of ten officers including Riley's team, left Thames House around 5.30 p.m. They arrived in the Sanderstead area just before 7.00 p.m. having battled their way through heavy rush hour traffic. Using their blue lights and sirens had helped keep them moving. However, they'd been on silent running for some time to mask their approach to the address Riley had given them.

The house was in a leafy suburb of London. All the houses where huge and worth around three quarters of a million pounds. At the end of the street was a large retirement home. The convoy pulled into the grounds and parked up. Martin went in and explained they needed to use the car park for the next six hours. The staff agreed as soon as he showed them his MI5 identification. The house was about four hundred yards from the retirement home. The road dipped in the middle and rose steeply at each end so they had a clear view from the home to the property Riley would enter.

Riley used the back of the command vehicle to spin invisible, just as she'd done in Washington. She then set off down the hill towards the house. Alex watched her through binoculars.

'Can you see where she is?' asked Martin.

'Yes, both Casey and I can see her when she's invisible,' replied Alex.

'Where is she now?' asked Martin.

'Sat on the front wall outside the house,' said Alex.

Riley radioed in to say everything seemed quiet. It stayed that way until nearly half past eight when suddenly teenagers started appearing in droves from both directions along the street. Casey tapped Alex on the shoulder as some walked past the gate of the retirement home.

'What is it?' he asked.

'These kids are dressed for a party, not a terrorist cell meeting,' she said.

Alex looked. 'Yeah, you're right,' he said.

He spoke to Martin and radioed Riley to abort the mission. However, Riley had watched a number of teenagers walk right past her into the house and her gut instinct was telling her to go in.

'Negative,' she replied. 'I think we should still go in. Karen has just arrived with those two boys from her class. Why don't you and Casey lose the body armour and gate crash like ordinary teenagers? The three of us can look around then,' she added.

Alex ran the idea by Martin, who reluctantly agreed to let them try.

'Keep an earpiece in though as I want communications kept open,' he said.

'Of course,' said Alex.

Chapter 14

The Party

Alex and Casey took off their body armour and walked down the road to join Riley.

'I'm not exactly dressed for a party,' said Casey.

'Me neither,' said Riley.

'Yeah, but I'm not invisible!' said Casey, smiling.

'Come on, you two, let's go,' said Alex.

The three of them entered the property unchallenged. There were so many teenagers in the house that three more would go unnoticed, even if just two of them were visible!

Casey grabbed some drinks and gave one to Alex.

'Remember, we're on duty,' said Alex.

'I'm blending in,' replied Casey.

'Let's split up and take a look around,' said Riley. 'Radio if you see anything.'

The three of them started to look around the house. Casey went out the back, Alex looked around downstairs and Riley went upstairs. There was loud music playing throughout the house, although upstairs was a bit quieter. Outside some partygoers were in bikinis in the swimming pool, others were standing around drinking. Downstairs, Alex found some guys playing pool.

Riley made her way along the landing upstairs. She opened a bedroom door to find two people making out on the bed. Apologising, she shut the door, then remembered they couldn't see or hear her anyway. Moving further along the landing she noticed a number of teenagers seemed to be going into one bedroom.

That's unusual, she thought, *normally these rooms are like the one I've just left!* She decided to radio the others. They met her at the top of the stairs.

'So, what's going on, Riley?' asked Casey.

'I'm not too sure, but several teenagers have gone in that

end room and no-one has come out,' she replied.

'What do you want to do?' said Alex.

'I wanna go in and see what's happening,' replied Riley.

'Let me radio control,' said Alex. He spoke to Martin for a minute and it was agreed Riley could enter.

'We will wait here and only come in if you're in trouble,' said Alex.

'Okay,' said Riley as she headed off towards the door. She decided to open it wide, walk in, then leave it as if someone outside had pushed it and run off.

As she entered, one of the kids inside said, 'What the hell!' Jumping to his feet, he looked out of the door.

Alex and Casey were talking at the far end of the landing and other kids were sitting on the floor in various places drinking and talking. Unable to pin blame on anyone for opening the door, the kid simply closed it and sat back down.

'What was that all about, Matty?' said another boy.

'No idea,' replied Matty.

Riley looked around. She noticed Amy and Karen were both in the room and a few other kids she didn't know. Then she spotted the man sat on a chair in the corner. It was the first and only adult she'd seen in the house and he looked creepy just sat there amongst all these teenagers. He looked like he was in his late twenties or early thirties.

The man stood up.

'Sit down, Matty, we're wasting time. I wanna thank Amy for the party, great cover for our meeting,' he said.

'No problem,' said Amy.

'The police are watching our normal place,' he said, 'so we need to change venue every time we meet now.' He paused then continued. 'So, you all know the plan. We will be coordinating our attack with the one in the American capital. Please tell me you've all put your packs somewhere safe.'

'Yes, sir,' came a corporate reply.

Riley, realising she'd found the other FWO cell, quickly took out her phone and started to photograph and record what was going on. She was there for nearly an hour. Alex hadn't risked the radio in case it gave away Riley's position. Although the electrical field that made her invisible generally prevented sound as well, he didn't want to risk it. When the group started to leave the room, Riley was about to follow them out when she noticed Amy was staying in the room with the older man. Riley decided to stay and see what happened next.

'Come here, you,' the man said to Amy.

'I'm coming, Ryan,' she said, as she walked across the room.

Riley watched as Ryan grabbed her and pulled her onto his lap. She seemed to go willingly. Riley watched as he started to kiss her. He moved his hand to touch her but she stopped him.

'Not here, Ryan, not with my school friends in the next room,' she said.

'Okay, fine,' he said angrily, pushing her off his lap. She fell on the floor. Getting up, she brushed herself off and walked away.

'Jerk,' she said under her breath as she walked past Riley towards the door.

Riley followed her out of the room where she rejoined Alex and Casey.

'I think we've got everything we are going to get here,' she said.

'Okay,' said Alex, 'let's get going.'

They went downstairs. Just as they reached the bottom, Karen stepped in front of them.

'Hey, I know you two, you started in my school this week from Canada or something,' she said.

'America,' replied Casey.

'What are you doing at this party?' said Karen.

'Leaving,' said Casey.

'I don't think so,' said Karen, putting her arm out to block their way.

Casey looked at Alex then back at Karen.

'Who invited you?' said Karen.

'Some kid at school,' said Alex.

'I don't think so,' replied Karen. 'I know every kid here and none of them would invite strangers to this party.'

'Well we don't know anyone here because we're new to the school,' said Casey, 'which is why we're going.'

By now their altercation had drawn a small crowd making the situation all the more difficult.

'We need to leave,' whispered Casey into her headset. Riley and Alex heard her, and Riley replied.

'Do you want me to move her out of the way?' she said.

'Let's keep you a secret if we can,' whispered Alex.

'What are you two mumbling about?' said Karen.

'Nothing,' said Casey, pushing Karen to one side and walking off.

Alex quickly realised that was his cue and followed suit. Amy came over and asked Karen what was going on.

'Oh, nothing, just those dumb exchange students gate crashing. I threw them out,' she said, which she clearly hadn't.

Out on the street, Alex, Casey and Riley made their way, at their fastest walking pace, down the road and up to the retirement home. Once there, Riley reappeared in the back of the command vehicle.

'Okay, Riley, what have you got for us?' asked Martin. Riley took out her phone and connected it to the onboard computer system. As the pictures and film uploaded, she put names to as many faces as she could. Then Ryan's picture uploaded. As it did, an MI5 file appeared on screen. Martin sat up in his chair.

'Hold on,' he said, 'this guy is known to us.' They watched as Martin opened the file.

'Ryan Peters,' he said, 'wanted by Interpol for murder in Greece, Spain and France. This guy is a contract killer, a mercenary. What is he doing organising an FWO cell?'

Martin turned to Riley.

'Did they say when or where the next meeting would be or anything about their plans for the 4th July?' he asked.

'Yes,' said Riley, 'they are meeting once more on the

night of the 3rd. Apparently, all the cell members have packs ready and hidden for use in the attack.'

'What is in these packs?' asked Martin.

'I'm not one hundred percent sure,' she replied, 'but if this cell has the same modus operandi as the Washington one then it'll be elements of a large explosive they plan to assemble inside your parliament.'

'Where's the next meeting happening?' asked Martin.

'In school,' replied Riley.

'Let's head back to Thames House,' said Martin, 'it's getting late.'

They sat down and buckled up. The journey back into the city didn't take quite as long this time as much of the traffic had cleared. Once they arrived at MI5 H.Q., Martin passed all their intel over to his Section Chief. Katy suggested the team stand down for the night and meet again on Sunday morning. So, Martin took James, Riley, Casey and Alex back to their hotel.

Although it was late, the hotel was very accommodating and provided the four of them with a meal. By the time they sat down to eat, it was nearly midnight.

'Wow, I can't believe how hungry I am,' said Casey.

'Yeah, it's been a long day,' said Riley.

'Well I expect the next few days will all be busy ones,' said Alex. 'So we're probably best heading to bed when we're finished.'

A short time later, Riley was in her room. Sitting at her dressing table, she picked up her brush and brushed her hair. She dragged the brush through a tangle of curls. Some relented and let her through. Others jammed the brush, pulling her hair. Eventually she won the battle and her hair felt soft and free again. She placed the brush back on the dresser and walked over to the bed. Pulling her pyjama vest and shorts from under the pillow she placed them on the duvet and started to take off her clothes. It felt so nice to finally be getting into bed. As usual, she pulled the covers right up, cocooning herself inside. She flicked a switch on her bedside table that turned off all the lights in the room.

At last the day was done. She closed her eyes and was soon fast asleep.

Chapter 15

Developments Stateside

Across the Atlantic, preparations were underway to stop the destruction of the US Capitol. With the intelligence provided by Riley, Casey and Alex, a team lead by the Secret Service was developing their plan.

FBI Director Jackson arrived at the Capitol Building and made his way up the steps to the entrance.

'Morning, Luca,' said Secret Service Director Andrews.

'Morning, Jack,' replied Luca. 'Are we meeting the Speaker of the House in her office?'

'Yes, as far as I'm aware,' replied Director Andrews. The two men entered the Capitol and approached the reception desk.

'Good morning gentlemen, welcome to the Capitol,' said the receptionist. 'How can I assist you this morning?'

'We are here to see Speaker O'Neil,' said Jack.

'Hold on one moment, sir,' said the receptionist. 'Who should I say is here for her?'

'The Directors of the FBI and the Secret Service,' replied Jack.

Once they'd got past reception, they went through Capitol security and up to the Speaker's office.

'Come in, gentlemen,' said Cynthia O'Neil. 'What can I do for you both?'

Jack and Luca came in and sat down in front of the Speaker's desk.

'Sorry to disturb you on a Saturday, Speaker O'Neil,' said Jack.

'Cynthia, please,' interrupted Cynthia.

'Very well, Cynthia,' continued Jack, 'but we need to bring a serious security matter to your attention.'

They went on to share their intelligence findings with the Speaker and what they knew about the nature of the attack that was coming. They also briefed her on Operation Legion and the joint Secret Service/MI5 Taskforce.

'We have a plan for the 4th July,' said Director Jackson.

'Yes,' said Director Andrews, 'but we will need the help of Congressional and Senate leadership to pull this off.'

'What exactly are you planning?' asked Speaker O'Neil.

'We want to create the illusion of normality within the Capitol on the 4th with everyone going about their normal business,' said Luca. 'But in reality, there won't be a single member of Congress, including the Senate, in the entire building.'

'This way, our government is protected if the attackers were to succeed,' added Jack.

'And who are you going to replace the 435 Congressmen and women, plus the 100 Senators, with?' asked Speaker O'Neil.

'With FBI agents, ma'am,' replied Luca.

'I appreciate you're trying to protect us, and I presume Operation Legion is classified. So how are you going to keep something like this quiet?' asked the Speaker.

'Everyone will be assigned an agent. We've identified members of my staff that are closest in appearance to each and every member of Congress. These agents will all accompany you to your homes on the 3rd of July and replace you on your normal journey to the Capitol the following day,' replied Luca.

'We'd also like you to give as many of your staff teams as possible leave that day, to minimise the risk. This should be easier to explain as it is Independence Day and I'm sure you get inundated with holiday requests.'

'We are,' replied the Speaker, 'however, we have a bigger problem. There will be thousands of members of the public there for the Capitol Fourth Concert Celebrations.'

'Yes, ma'am, we are well aware of that and we think that's why the FWO has chosen that day for the attack,' said Director Andrews.

'But with so many people around, the Capitol Police will be on high alert. Surely that'll make it harder for the terrorist cell?' suggested the Speaker.

'In many ways you're right, but the reality is, if they're determined enough, they'll try and find a way through,' said Director Jackson.

'What should I tell my people for now?' asked the Speaker.

'Just start by getting as many people on leave from work to reduce the risk in the Capitol Building for now and we will sort the rest,' replied Director Jackson.

When they left her office, they made their way through the building to speak with the Head of the Capitol Police. They decided not to share their plans for the Congressmen and women but did bring the police up to speed on the terrorists' plan.

The sun rose early on the Sunday morning. It gleamed through the thin curtains in Riley's London hotel room. As the light twinkled on the pillow next to her, she lay watching it. It made her think of the shimmer from her skin when she was invisible. She wondered what her life would be like now if she'd not been struck by lightning, or saved the President from assassination. The idea of being that lonely, bullied girl again sent a shiver down her spine. She wasn't going back to sleep after that thought, she'd have nightmares! So reluctantly, she pulled back the covers and sat up. Looking at the clock, she discovered it was still quite early. *Well, I'm not going to sleep any more,* she thought to herself. Swinging her legs out of bed, she stood up on the soft carpet and made her way across the room to the little kettle. Making herself a coffee, she sat back down on her bed. She picked up her sketchbook and continued working on the portrait of Alex.

The Washington bookstore was closed today which was perfect for Chris Cannons. He arrived early in the hope of getting inside undetected. Unfortunately for him, since Riley's first visit to the bookstore, the FBI had put surveillance on the building 24/7.

'Hey, roll the film,' said one the agents on the second floor of the building opposite. 'I think that's Cannons.'

The other agent got out of his chair, flicked a switch on their recording equipment and came over to look through the binoculars.

Once inside the bookstore, Cannons waited for various accomplices to arrive.

'Is everything set?' he asked.

'Yeah, boss, of course,' replied one of his goons. Cannons smiled.

'The FBI are such idiots if they think we don't know they're watching us,' he said.

'What are we gonna do about the Security Services?' asked another goon.

'It's all been taken care of,' said Cannons. 'My man on the inside told me the FBI came to see the Capitol Police yesterday.'

'Isn't that gonna cause us trouble?' said the first goon.

'Possibly,' said Cannons, 'we may need to change our plans. My man on the inside will make sure we know what's possible before we decide on anything.'

'What's the latest from London?' asked the second goon?'

'They're all set. They've even issued the kids with their packs,' replied Cannons.

'Wow, that's risky,' said one of the goons.

'Yeah, well, that's their look out,' replied Cannons. 'We will stick to our plan and hand the stuff out on Thursday night,' he added.

One of the men with Cannons looked over at the packs in the corner of the room.

'So how do they work, boss?' he asked.

'They're a clever design,' replied Cannons. 'Each backpack has a shielded compartment in its base which contains a different element of a bomb. Each kid will carry one pack and a USB cable, which looks like a phone charger. Once in position all the packs are joined together by the cables and then I can remotely detonate,' he said.

'That's some quality gear,' replied the goon.

'It is indeed,' said Cannons.

The two agents in the building opposite forwarded the images they'd got that morning of the various cell members entering the bookstore. They'd heard back from H.Q. and weren't surprised to read that they were all white supremacists known to the FBI. As the day progressed, various members of the cell left the bookstore. However, Chris Cannons never reappeared. The FBI assumed he must be staying on site. Their assumptions were wrong!

There was a knock at Riley's hotel room door. She put her sketchbook down, leaving it open, and went to the door. Looking through the spy hole, she saw Alex and Casey, still in their pyjamas outside. She opened the door.

'Morning, guys, come in,' she said. 'You up early too?'

'Yeah,' said Casey, 'too much going around my head to sleep.'

'Do you two want a coffee?' asked Riley.

'Yeah, that'd be great,' said Alex.

'Please,' added Casey.

Riley went to the kettle and switched it on. Alex noticed the open sketchbook on the bed.

'Hey, is this me?' he said.

Riley ran over and grabbed the sketchbook.

'You're not meant to have seen that yet, and yeah it's you,' she said.

'Where's mine?' said Casey, sounding disgruntled.

'I'll do yours too, don't worry,' said Riley, giving Casey a gentle, reassuring smile.

The three sat on the bed cross-legged in a circle with their coffees.

'So, what's causing the lack of sleep?' Alex asked Casey.

'Oh, just the usual stuff, like can we really pull this off and stop the bad guys,' replied Casey.

'I know what you mean,' said Riley, 'this is so much bigger than Joe and his assassination attempt on the

President.'

'It is,' said Alex, 'but the difference now is we've been trained, we have backup and we aren't working alone anymore.'

'Yeah, that's true,' said Casey.

'See,' said Riley, 'nothing to worry about!'

'Do either of you know what's happening today?' asked Casey.

'No idea,' said Riley.

Just as she finished speaking someone knocked at the door. Riley went to see who it was.

'It's James,' she said, looking through the spy hole.

'Well let him in!' said Casey. Riley opened the door and James walked in.

'There you all are,' he said. 'Get yourselves up and dressed and come down for breakfast, will you?'

Alex and Casey got up from Riley's bed and went back to their rooms.

'I'll see you all downstairs in half an hour,' James said to them all as he left Riley to get dressed. Once they'd sorted themselves out, they made their way to the breakfast buffet in the hotel's dining room and found James sat at a table.

'Grab some food, guys, then come and join me,' he said.

They all sat down with the various plates and drinks they'd gathered from the buffet.

'So, what's happening?' asked Riley.

Chapter 16

Time Off

As they ate their breakfast James explained that they were going to spend the week back in the London High School to see if they could gather any more intelligence from Karen and the others. He told them he would be visiting the Houses of Parliament with Martin and Section Chief Roberts to conduct a risk assessment based on the intelligence they currently had.

'So, do you think we can stop this from happening?' asked Casey.

'I think so,' said James. 'The FWO don't know how much intel we have or that Riley has been sat in the cell meetings on both sides of the Atlantic. That gives us a real advantage.'

'Let's hope so,' said Riley.

'You've got a break today,' said James. 'Not standard protocol on a mission like this, but you guys are not a standard team and bosses from the Secret Service and MI5 have decided you need to be teenagers for the day.'

'So, what does that mean?' asked Alex.

'It means you can have the rest of the day out in London as long as you behave yourselves and don't draw any attention,' replied James. 'Just be back at the hotel for dinner at 8.00 p.m. You'll be back in school in the morning.'

'Fantastic,' said Casey, 'I've always wanted to look round London.'

The three of them finished their breakfast and went back to their rooms to get ready. They met back in the hotel lobby around 10.00 a.m. and set off to explore London.

'Where shall we go first?' said Alex.

'The London Eye,' said the girls at the same time!

'Well that was freaky,' said Casey.

'You mean you two didn't plan that?' said Alex.

'Nope, pure coincidence,' said Riley.

'Okay,' said Alex, 'the London Eye it is!'

They made their way on the London Underground to Waterloo Station and walked through the backstreets towards the river. The Ferris wheel was huge. They walked over to the ticket office to see if they could buy a ticket.

'Sorry,' said the clerk, 'you need to book months in advance for this attraction.'

'That's a shame,' said Riley, 'we're only here for the day and only found out we weren't working an hour ago.'

'Hold on a moment,' said the clerk. She went to the back of the ticket office, then reappeared moments later.

'Don't tell anyone, as these are normally held back for VIPs,' she said, handing them three tickets for the 11.00 a.m. slot.

'Thank you,' said Riley, 'how much do we owe you?'

'Oh, it's okay, you can have these on me. Just don't tell the world!' replied the clerk.

'Wow, thanks,' they all replied and headed off to join the queue for the wheel.

Once on board they found a good spot in the huge glass pod and watched as it slowly moved, lifting them up higher and higher.

'Look,' said Casey, pointing, 'there's the Houses of Parliament. I can't believe someone wants to destroy that!'

'Casey! Shhhh,' said Riley, 'keep your voice down!'

'Oops, sorry,' said Casey.

The Eye took about half an hour to go right round. It gave them a chance to have a good look across the city and decide on some places they wanted to see.

As they left the London Eye, Alex asked, 'So, are we going to Buckingham Palace next?'

'Sounds like a plan,' said Riley.

'Then Trafalgar Square,' said Casey.

'How about a break for a coffee before that?' suggested Riley.

'That sounds good,' said Alex, 'we don't want to exhaust ourselves.'

They went back to Waterloo and took the tube to Green Park. It didn't take long to walk to the Palace from there. As they stood at the main gates and looked in, they wondered what it must be like to live in such a huge house.

'I expect the Queen doesn't use half of the place,' said Casey.

'Bet she's glad she doesn't have to clean it!' said Riley. Alex didn't comment. He was busy watching the guards marching back and forth.

'They're so disciplined,' he said.

'Who are?' asked Casey, distracted by his comment.

'The guards,' replied Alex.

'Oh, yeah, I guess they have to be,' said Casey.

'Come on, you two, let's go and find somewhere for a drink,' interjected Riley.

They headed off down the Mall towards Admiralty Arch and Whitehall. It took them some time but eventually they'd worked their way round to Trafalgar Square, where they stopped for a coffee and a rest.

'I don't think I've walked that far since the three of us walked from Union Station to the White House that day,' said Riley.

'Yeah, me neither, let's stay here for a bit,' said Casey.

'Fine with me,' said Alex, 'but afterwards we are going to Covent Garden to see the street entertainment.'

'How do you know about that?' asked Riley.

Alex waved a leaflet he'd been looking at on the table. After an hour or so, they left the cafe and made their way through the streets from Trafalgar Square to Covent Garden. There they found the old covered market place with its quaint little shops and boutiques. And sure enough, on nearly every street corner was a juggler, comedian, magician or the like. They stopped to watch several shows before deciding their legs needed another rest.

Sitting down in a cafe near Leicester Square, they checked the time.

'Wow, it's nearly 5.00 p.m.,' said Casey, 'and we've not been to Harrods, Oxford Street or...' Riley stopped her.

'There isn't time for everything, Casey,' she said.

'We could fit in one more thing before going back to the hotel,' said Alex, 'and I've got a suggestion.' The girls looked at him.

'Go on then,' said Casey.

'The Tower of London,' said Alex.

'I don't want to visit some skyscraper!' said Casey. Riley and Alex burst out laughing!

'What?' said Casey.

'The Tower of London is a castle that houses the Crown Jewels,' said Riley.

'Oh,' said Casey, turning a deep shade of red.

'I think it would be a good reminder of what we are trying to protect in this country. Besides the US has nothing like it so it'd be cool to see,' said Alex.

'I'm in,' said Riley.

'Me too,' said Casey.

Once they'd finished their drinks, they made their way from Leicester Square to Tower Hill Station.

On arrival at the Tower of London they discovered the last tour had finished. The Tower was open but the Crown Jewels were not.

'That's disappointing,' said Alex. The clerk asked where they'd come from, recognising their accents.

'Washington DC,' said Casey. 'We only have the day too, as we head back soon.' The clerk left the desk.

'Please tell me we can pull this off twice in one day!' said Alex, referring to them accessing the London Eye without booking tickets.

On her return, the clerk had a guard in a strange uniform.

'This is one of the Queen's Beefeaters,' she said. 'They're about to lock the Crown Jewels away, but if you go with him, he will let you see them, briefly!'

'That's awesome, thank you, ma'am,' said Riley.

They followed the Beefeater across the castle grounds to the central tower and inside.

'You can only be here for two minutes,' he said, 'and no photographs.'

'Yes, sir,' they all replied.

Suddenly there they were. Sealed in a glass security case, behind a barrier was the Queen's crown and various other glistening jewels.

'Wow,' said Casey, 'they're incredible.'

'Aren't they?' said the Beefeater, 'and worth millions.'

'No wonder you take such good care to protect them,' said Alex.

At that moment, the girls realised why he'd wanted them to see this. This country had a rich history, which their country was a part of, and they had a role now to protect both.

'Thank you so much for showing us this,' said Alex, as the Beefeater escorted them back to the Tower's main reception.

'My pleasure, young man,' said the Beefeater, 'enjoy the rest of your time in London.'

They looked at each other, all thinking that wasn't really an option.

When they left the Tower of London it was time to head back to the hotel. Sitting on the hot crowded tube train, Riley said, 'I can't believe that day went so fast.'

'Fun days always do,' said Casey.

'It was good fun, wasn't it?' said Alex.

'Yeah it was,' said Riley. 'I'm glad we were given some time to enjoy our friendship before you know what!'

'Hey, this is our stop,' said Alex.

'Excuse me,' they said, as they pushed their way through the cramped carriage and out onto the busy platform.

'Boy, I'm glad to be outta there!' said Casey. 'I know how a sardine feels squashed in a tin now!'

It didn't take them long to reach the hotel. They found James sat in the hotel bar.

'Hi, you three. Have a good day?' he asked.

'Yeah, great thanks,' replied Alex.

'So, what did you get up to?' asked James.

'Well, we've been on the London Eye, visited Buckingham Palace, Trafalgar Square, Leicester Square,

Covent Garden and seen the Crown Jewels at the Tower of London!' said Casey.

'Wow!' said James, 'you must be exhausted!'

'Just a bit,' said Riley, plonking herself in a nearby chair.

'Do you want to freshen up before dinner or go straight in?' asked James.

'Can we go straight in?' said Riley. 'I'm actually quite hungry after all that.'

'Fine with us,' said the others. So they found a table and ordered.

After dinner Riley went to her room. She really wanted a shower as her skin felt sticky or dirty from being on tube trains and around the city all day. However, she was also shattered, so decided the shower could wait until the morning. Putting on her pyjamas she climbed into bed. She didn't pull the covers over her as she was feeling hotter than usual which she put down to the day's activities. Lying there, she wondered if she'd sleep feeling this warm. She noticed a fan standing in the corner of the room. Getting up, she positioned it and switched in on. Lying back down, she could feel the cool air tickling her bare feet and legs as the fan turned from side to side. *That's better,* she thought. It didn't take long before her eyes were closed and she was fast asleep.

Chapter 17

Some Old School Issues

Riley was woken by her alarm on Monday morning. Still feeling tired from her day sightseeing in London, she forced herself out of bed and into the shower. Glad to finally be clean and fresh from the city dirt, she rubbed her skin dry with the soft towel. It didn't take her long to get dressed and join the others for breakfast.

'What time is Martin coming?' asked Riley.

'In about half an hour,' replied James, 'so eat up, as you can't be late.'

'Don't forget to turn invisible after breakfast,' said Casey to Riley.

'Good point, it's been a few days since I last did that. Easy to forget!'

'How on earth can you forget you have the power of invisibility?' said Alex.

'I don't mean that,' said Riley. 'Because you guys can see me either way, I forget whether I'm visible or not when I'm with you. It's nice actually, knowing I'm just me around you.'

'Don't go getting all mushy on us,' said Casey laughing.

'Very funny,' replied Riley.

'Right, you three go and get your school stuff,' said James. 'Martin will be here any minute.'

Sure enough, when they arrived back in the hotel lobby Martin was waiting.

'Is Riley with you?' asked Martin.

'Yeah she's here,' said Casey, smiling.

'What are you smiling at?' asked Martin.

'Oh, it's just Agent Jacobs used to ask us that every morning in DC when we were undercover in a school there!' replied Casey.

'Ah, fair enough,' said Martin. 'Come on then, let's get

going.'

The journey to school didn't take long and they were soon standing in the crowded corridor with kids all around them battling to reach lockers before the inevitable bell rang out.

'I swear every high school is the same mad frenzy first thing,' said Casey as she slammed her locker shut.

'Come on,' said Alex, 'let's get to registration.'

As they walked into the classroom, they saw Karen, with her little crowd of followers talking by the window. Alex and Casey found their seats and Riley perched herself on the front of the teacher's desk.

'Sit down everyone!' announced the teacher as she walked in. 'Right, let's get the register done so you can get to your classes,' she added.

As the names were called, Riley noticed there was no Amy in class. She wondered if she was okay after the way Ryan had treated her at the party.

Once registration was finished, the class headed out to their first lesson. As they went, Riley noticed Karen breaking off from the main group and heading down a different corridor. She seemed to be busy texting someone. Riley got close to Alex and said she'd catch up later as she was going to follow Karen.

'Okay,' replied Alex.

Riley followed close behind Karen. She couldn't quite see over her shoulder to find out who it was she was texting. At the end of the corridor, Karen turned and went through a door into the girls' bathroom. Riley followed her inside. The sight that greeted her was not what she expected. Standing in the corner of the room, half hidden in the shadows, was Amy.

'Hey,' said Karen, 'how you doing?' Amy stepped out of the shadows. As she did, the shock of what she saw made Riley put her hand over her open mouth to muffle the sound of a gasp.

Amy was standing there in her underwear, her skin covered in cuts and bruises.

'Oh my God! Amy!' said Karen. 'What has happened to you?' Karen rushed over to hug her friend. Amy just stood there crying.

'Was this Ryan?' asked Karen.

'Yes,' said Amy through the tears.

'Let me help you,' said Karen, getting some clean tissue and wetting it under a tap. She cleaned Amy's wounds and helped her get dressed.

'We need to tell someone about this,' said Karen.

'We can't,' said Amy, 'it'll put the mission at risk and we can't do that.'

'Well we need to keep you away from him until this is all over,' said Karen.

'Okay,' said Amy.

'Let's get out of here,' said Karen.

The two of them left the bathroom. Riley followed them until they reached the main door of the school then watched as they left the grounds of the school together. Riley decided to stay and catch up with Casey and Alex.

She found them in the school Art room half way through a lesson.

'Hey,' said Riley,

'Oh, hi, how did you get on?' asked Casey.

'Not good,' said Riley. 'I followed Karen to the bathroom where she met with Amy.'

'I thought Amy wasn't in school,' said Alex.

'So did I,' said Riley.

Riley went on to explain about cuts and bruises and how Amy had got them.

'We need to do something about this!' she concluded.

'I agree with what you're saying and your reason for saying it, but we need to consider what we are dealing with here,' said Alex.

'What do you mean?' asked Riley.

'Look, I know you want to help. You hate seeing anyone bullied or abused, but Ryan isn't a school bully. He's a mercenary wanted by the British Secret Service and Interpol. Also, Amy, although the same age as us, is in fact a suspected terrorist,' said Alex.

'I know all that,' said Riley, 'but it doesn't make what he did right.'

'True,' said Casey, 'but we'd need MI5's approval to act on this and I don't think they'll allow it four days before Operation Legion.'

'I guess you're both right,' said Riley. 'It's just frustrating not being able to help.'

'Look,' said Alex, 'run it by Martin later. The worst he can say is no!'

They decided to leave the matter for Martin to advise them on later and got on with the rest of the school day. Riley managed to follow Matty around in the afternoon. He was one of the boys from the party. However, he had an ordinary day at school and didn't offer up any new intel for Riley and her team.

At the end of the day the three of them left the school to meet Martin who was waiting to take them to their hotel. Alex explained in the car that Riley wanted to talk with him, so Martin came into the hotel. Riley used the bar toilets to spin visible and then sat down with Martin to share what had happened with Karen and Amy that morning.

'I'm afraid your friends are right, there's not a lot we can do this close to Operation Legion,' he said. 'However, if you see Amy or anyone else being assaulted you can directly intervene and use your powers, but only if the situation doesn't put you at risk.'

Riley seemed frustrated by this, but she realised there was a lot at stake with their mission. She decided to stick by Amy at school to see if she needed help.

As they arrived at school the following morning, they saw Amy walking in with Karen.

'At least she's coming to school,' said Casey.

'You still planning to shadow her?' Alex asked Riley.

'Yeah, if that's okay with you guys,' replied Riley.

'Of course,' said Alex, 'just let us know if there's anything we can do.'

'Thanks, I will,' said Riley.

After registration Amy headed off to her Games lesson with Karen and a few others. The class all did different subjects based on their exam choices, so not everyone had sports that day. Riley went with Amy's group, trying to listen to the conversation as she went.

'So, did you see him yesterday?' asked Karen.

'No,' replied Amy, 'I told him I don't want any more to do with him.'

'Well done you,' said Karen.

'Yeah it felt good to say it,' said Amy, 'but I'm scared what he might do. It's not like we can avoid him, is it?'

'True,' said Karen, 'but you have friends that will look out for you.'

Riley was pleased to hear Karen say this. It was hard seeing these guys in their day-to-day lives, knowing they were terror suspects.

Once they were changed, Karen and Amy made their way to the sports hall with the other girls. They spent the next hour playing basketball, which Amy was surprisingly good at, in Riley's opinion anyway. As the lesson drew to an end, the games teacher blew her whistle and directed the girls back to the changing rooms. By the time Riley walked in, girls were already stepping out of the showers to get themselves dried and dressed.

Amy was a little slower, perhaps because the water was hurting her cuts and bruises, or because she waited to shower after the others had finished. It would be easier to avoid comments and questions that way. Riley recognised the behaviour as it was the sort of thing she used to do at school. As a result, most of the girls were done when Amy started to get changed.

The teacher came out of her room and said, 'Are you not done, Amy?'

'No, Miss,' she replied.

'Very well,' said the teacher, 'here's my key. Lock the changing rooms when you're done and take the key to the staff room.'

'Yes, Miss,' she said.

Karen had left and Amy was now alone. Suddenly the door from the back of the changing area opened and in walked Ryan. Amy, who only had her underwear on at this point grabbed her wet towel and held it in front of herself.

'What the hell are you doing here?' she said.

'I'm here to see you, babe,' replied Ryan.

'I'm not your babe, and how the hell did you get into school undetected?' she replied.

'I do this for a living, remember! I can get anywhere I want,' he said.

'Good,' she replied, 'you can get the hell out of here then!'

Riley was impressed with Amy's confidence, although she could hear how terrified Amy was from her voice.

'I'm not going anywhere,' replied Ryan, stepping closer to her.

Amy backed away, although there wasn't much room to do so as the bench containing her clothes was just behind her. Ryan grabbed her towel and pulled it away from her.

'Come here, babe!' he said.

'No, leave me alone, you psycho!' she screamed at him.

Riley realised she had to act. Raising her hand, she focussed and released an energy pulse that pushed Ryan across the room to the far wall and held him there.

Amy watched as he glided backwards away from her and then just stood pressed against the wall unable to move.

'What the hell is going on?' he shouted.

Having no idea how to answer, but realising she had moments to escape, Amy grabbed her clothes and shoes and ran from the changing room into the school corridor. When she got there, she realised she was still just wearing her underwear. Fortunately, the corridor was empty, except for Karen.

'What the blazes!' said Karen.

'Ryan's in there,' replied Amy in a panicked voice as she put her shirt back on.

'Come on,' said Karen, 'let's get away from here.'

Back in the changing room, Riley was still holding Ryan

against the wall. She increased the energy pulse and moved him along the wall towards the open door he'd entered by. As he reached it, she pushed him through and he fell to the ground. She rushed forward, pulled the door shut and locked it. Then, wasting no time, she went through the changing room and out of the other door into the corridor. It was empty with no sign of Amy, Karen or anyone else.

Chapter 18

Security Breach

Riley headed off down the corridor to try and find Alex and Casey. She knew their next class was Geography so it was just a case of finding the right room. It took her a while but she eventually tracked them down to a first-floor classroom.

'Hi, you two, you'll never guess what just happened!' said Riley.

'What?' asked Alex.

'Amy was the last to leave the changing rooms, like after the teacher had gone,' she said, 'and before she could leave, Ryan walked in. How he got in the school I don't know.'

'Oh my, what happened?' said Casey in an anxious voice.

'He went for Amy. I used my energy pulse and pushed him across the room and pinned him to the wall,' replied Riley.

'I'd like to have seen that!' said Casey.

'Yeah his face was a picture, he'd got no idea what was happening to him,' said Riley.

'Then what happened?' asked Alex.

'Amy grabbed her things and ran out of the changing room and I used the energy pulse to push Ryan through the open door before I shut him out.'

'Nice one,' said Casey.

'Do you know where Amy or indeed Ryan are now?' asked Alex.

'No, sorry, I lost sight of both of them,' replied Riley.

Karen took Amy to the bathroom so she could finish getting dressed with at least some privacy.

'We should report this to the office. He shouldn't be in the school,' said Karen.

Amy reluctantly agreed and the two of them headed to

the administration office once she was dressed.

'I want to track Amy down at break time and check she's okay,' said Riley.

'I'm sure she will be if Karen is staying with her,' said Alex.

Suddenly an alarm sounded and an announcement came over the school tannoy system.

'The school is in lockdown,' said the administrator's voice.

'I need to get out of here,' said Riley, 'I can't do anything trapped in a classroom.'

Before the others could speak Riley had bolted for the door and just made it through as the teacher shut and locked it. Flicking off the classroom light she ordered all the pupils onto the floor and under desks.

'This isn't a planned practice,' she said, 'so I want absolute silence in here.' She sounded very serious so everyone, surprisingly, obeyed.

Out in the corridor. Riley came across a couple of teachers. Then she saw the Head going to the main entrance of the school. She decided to follow. At the main door the Head let several police officers in.

'Apparently he's somewhere in the building. Last seen in the girls' changing rooms,' said the Head.

'Okay, leave it to us,' said one of the officers.

Riley decided to go it alone and started to search the school herself. There didn't seem to be any sign of Ryan and she started to wonder if he'd left after being pushed out of the changing room door. She went outside, heading past police and teachers in several corridors. Walking past the changing block and the sports hall, she noticed a split in the fence. Then out of nowhere Ryan appeared and dashed towards the fence. Riley was left to make a snap decision. Should she stop him and have the police question him for several days, or let him go and not put Operation Legion at risk. She recalled what her friends had said earlier and decided to let him slip away quietly – this time!

After a thorough search, the police said there was no-one

on site, but did tell the Head about the split in the fence. The lockdown was lifted and normal school resumed. When the lunch break started, Riley rejoined Casey and Alex in the canteen for something to eat.

'What are you planning on doing this afternoon?' asked Casey.

'Finding Amy and Karen,' said Riley.

'I can do that for you now,' said Alex. 'They're sat over there,' he added, pointing at a table three rows away.

'Great, saves me wandering the corridors again,' replied Riley. 'What are you two going to do?'

'Alex and I are going to see if Matty and some of the others have any usable intel,' said Casey.

'Be careful,' said Riley. Casey laughed.

'What are you laughing at?' asked Riley.

'You're the one who singlehandedly fought a mercenary this morning and you're telling me to be careful!'

'Ah, I see your point,' said Riley, smiling.

That afternoon Riley followed Amy from lesson to lesson. She had several with Karen and they talked, but mainly about boys. Amy expressed how frustrated she was at getting involved with Ryan, how she wished he'd not been so violent with her.

'You are so outta that relationship after Friday,' said Karen.

'I hope you're right,' said Amy, not sounding so sure.

The day came to an end and Riley, Casey and Alex met up to go back to their hotel. They'd found out nothing new and the following day proved to be the same.

Riley's alarm woke her early on Thursday morning. She really didn't want to get up as she knew the day would be a long one. As she lay in bed, she thought about everything they'd done over the last few months: the training, the undercover assignments, discovering the ability to fly. They'd achieved so much. But now it would all come down to the next forty-eight hours and whether they could stop the First World Order.

Getting up from her bed, Riley made her way to her

bathroom and started to brush her teeth. About an hour later she arrived downstairs, having showered and dressed.

'Morning, everyone,' she said as she walked into the buffet area in the hotel dining room.

Alex, Casey and James were already eating their breakfast.

'Hi Riley, grab some food and join us,' said Casey.

After breakfast, Martin arrived to take them to school. On the way he told them he'd pick them up at lunchtime for a briefing at Thames House.

'I'll get you back in time for the after school FWO cell meeting,' he said.

'Okay Martin, we'll see you later,' said Alex as they got out of the car.

During the morning, Riley followed Karen and Amy around. She heard them talking with some other cell members about the meeting after school.

'So, it's in the girls' changing rooms then?' said one of the boys in a questioning manner.

'Yes, I copied the key. Amy was given it by a teacher this week,' said Karen.

'It's a good choice, because the room has no windows and no-one will expect people to meet there,' said Amy.

'What about after school sports clubs?' asked Matty.

'There aren't any today,' said Karen.

'What time do you want us there?' said another boy.

'As soon as school ends,' said Karen.

'Does Ryan know where to find us?' asked Matty.

'Oh yes,' said Amy, 'he knows exactly where to go!'

Martin arrived at the school for 12.00 noon. Riley, Casey and Alex were waiting for him.

'I'll have these two back as soon as I can,' he said to the administrator, referring to Alex and Casey.

He'd told the school office there was an issue with their visas which required a quick visit to the US Embassy.

When they arrived at Thames House they went straight to the briefing room where Riley spun herself visible. Once her brain burn had cleared, she was able to focus on the briefing which was already underway.

'Okay,' said Section Chief Roberts, 'we now have the names of all the cell members. Thanks to Riley we know the cell is meeting in three hours at the school. This is the last meeting planned before the attack. So, it will be crucial to get as much intel as possible.'

'Yes, ma'am,' said Riley.

'Here's what we know so far. The attack will happen around the same time in Washington and London. Because of the five-hour time difference and the fact that there is a major event in the Capitol tomorrow afternoon, we believe the attack will be around 5.00 p.m. here and 12.00–2.00 p.m. in DC,' said the Section Chief.

'Can we verify that?' asked James.

'I'm hoping today's meeting in the school will,' replied the Section Chief. 'We also know the terrorists have a bomb made up of various parts that can be connected using USB cables.'

'Yes, ma'am,' replied Martin, 'and we will be searching anyone arriving at Westminster tomorrow to see if they are carrying them.'

'What about school trips to Parliament?' asked Alex. 'Are there any booked for tomorrow?'

'Yes,' replied the Section Chief, 'but none from your school.'

'They could be using another school's trip as cover,' said James. 'I'll look into it.'

'Thank you,' said Section Chief Roberts.

'Riley, the plan is to have you and a team or officers inside Parliament. The Prime Minister has been briefed and is keeping the Cabinet members away until the crisis is over. I'll be wanting you to find the explosives, but then stand down and let our experts handle that,' said the Section Chief.

'I'm glad about that!' replied Riley.

'Okay, so let's meet again later once Riley has the intelligence from the next cell meeting,' said Section Chief Roberts.

'Yes, ma'am,' said everyone as they got up to leave.

Before heading back to school, Riley was kitted out with body armour and communications equipment. They then returned to school with Martin. Alex and Casey were told to report to the operation command vehicle as soon as school ended. It was positioned two blocks from the school. Riley was told to follow Amy and Karen to the cell meeting.

The bell soon rang out for the end of school. There was the usual mayhem at the lockers in the corridors which gave Amy and co the perfect cover to slip into the changing rooms unnoticed. Riley followed them in to find Ryan and several other adults already inside. Amy looked nervous around him. Riley noticed Karen was staying very close to Amy.

'Right, you lot, we've got loads to get through so settle down and shut up!' said Ryan.

Riley took out her phone, making sure she had a tight hold this time, and started to film the meeting.

'So, tomorrow's the big day,' said Ryan, 'and we are ready. Everything is in place thanks to our inside man. All the bomb parts are already in the parliament building ready for you to collect tomorrow. Well done all of you for looking after them and passing them on as instructed.'

Riley was feeling a bit confused. Did she miss that instruction? Maybe it was something the cell had planned before she was undercover. The main thing was she knew now!

'So,' Ryan continued, 'you'll collect your bags, take them to the House of Commons and leave them there assembled. You'll have one minute to get away once it's set.'

'That's not long,' said Matty.

'No, but any longer and security will have time to stop it from going boom!' said Ryan with an evil smirk on his face.

'Oh, also there's been a slight change of plan at the American end. Apparently, the FBI had a meeting with the Capitol Police about our comrades in DC. What they don't know is our man in the Capitol Police has told their entire plan to our comrades. They were going to attack the public celebration at the Capitol but the FBI are expecting that. So, they've moved their plans up. They can't attack too early or security will be too tight for us. So we've agreed, we attack at 3.00 p.m. and they'll attack at 10.00 a.m. which in reality is the same time!'

'What are they doing if they're not attacking the Independence Day celebrations?' asked Karen.

'They're planning to destroy the White House!' said Ryan. 'Anyway, enough about their mission and back to ours,' Ryan went on.

He told them what time to meet and where. He told them all to make their own way to school so parents didn't hold up the mission. He then dismissed them all except Amy. Karen stayed put as well.

'You can go, Karen,' said Ryan.

'Not without Amy,' she replied.

'We have things to talk about,' he said.

'It'll have to wait until tomorrow,' said Karen, grabbing Amy by the hand and pulling her through the door before he could stop them.

Looking very angry, Ryan got up and left through the back door with the other adults, leaving Riley standing there alone.

Chapter 19

The London Cell

Riley went to leave the changing rooms to find the door locked. Karen had locked it when she'd left. *Great,* thought Riley, *now I have to leave the same way as Ryan.* She went to the door she'd pushed him through a few days before to find that locked as well! *How? He must have a key as well,* she thought. There was only one thing for it. She'd have to blast the door with her energy pulse. Focusing on the back door, she raised her hand. An energy pulse burst forth and the door didn't move. 'What!' she said out loud. Deciding it needed to be much stronger, she focussed the kind of energy she used for flight. Aiming at the door again she fired her energy pulse and watched as the door disintegrated into a pile of match sticks. Hoping the noise hadn't drawn any unwanted attention, she slipped away to rejoin Casey and Alex and the MI5 officers.

Still holding Amy's hand, Karen ran across the school yard, almost dragging her friend. Only when they reached the school gate, did they pause for breath.

'That was a risky thing to do!' said Amy, 'but I'm glad you did it.'

'There was no way I was leaving you alone with him,' replied Karen.

'Thanks,' replied Amy, giving her friend a big hug.

'Come on,' said Karen, 'let's get out of here.'

Once inside the command vehicle, Riley spun visible again, trying her best not to smash the computers onboard the Transit van they were in.

'Hi, Riley,' said Martin. 'What do you have for us?'

'I have loads,' replied Riley, 'but we also have a major problem!'

Karen and Amy walked over the road and cut down behind the flats. There was a dual carriageway to cross next to the fire station. Once they were over that, they followed the back streets up the hill to the main road and the shops. They walked past the bottom of the market street on the way.

'Shouldn't we be going through the market?' asked Amy, knowing the bus stop was at the top.

'No not yet,' said Karen, 'we've got somewhere else to go first.'

Amy was just happy to be in Karen's company. She felt safe around Karen so followed her up the hill to the main shopping street.

'What's the problem?' asked Martin.

'There's been a major security breach in the US. The FWO know the plans for the American part of Operation Legion!' said Riley.

'Bloody hell!' said Alex.

Riley and Casey looked at him. They'd never heard him swear before so it was a bit of a shock!

'Okay,' said Martin, 'let's get back to Thames House as quick as possible. We are going to need the Director General's input on this one.'

Wasting no more time, he told them to strap in and climbed through to the driver's seat. Before they knew it, they were speeding through the London streets with the sirens blaring.

Amy and Karen where about to cross the road when the unmarked MI5 van shot past with its siren on.

'Wow, someone's in a hurry to get the tea on!' said Karen.

Amy laughed as the two of them crossed the road. They headed down a side road next to the large department store that dominated the high street.

'Here we are,' said Karen, taking Amy's hand and pulling her into a trendy little cafe.

They made their way to the sofas at the back of the cafe.

They sat together on the large one that faced the front of the cafe. From there they could see everything that was going on in the cafe. Amy watched as people went about their everyday lives. She wondered what her life would be like if she wasn't stuck in this relationship with Ryan.

'Hey, come on,' said Karen, handing her a menu, 'forget about him for five minutes and choose a drink!'

Amy gave a sigh and took the menu. *How did Karen know what she was thinking? Was her face that obvious?* she thought.

'Can I have a green tea?' she asked Karen.

'Yeah, sure, give me a minute,' said Karen getting up to go and order at the counter. When she returned, she was carrying a tray with a green tea and a cappuccino. The green tea was in a glass and you could see the teabag floating in the hot water. Karen placed the tray on the coffee table in front of them and sat herself back down.

Handing her friend the tea, she asked, 'So, how are you feeling about tomorrow?'

'Nervous,' replied Amy. 'What if we don't get out in time? Or if we get caught?' she said.

'Yeah, I've been having the exact same thoughts,' said Karen.

'Thing is, we're committed now,' said Amy. 'You know Ryan would hunt us down and kill us if we didn't show!'

'Yeah I know,' said Karen, her voice sounding burdened and weak.

'How the hell did we get mixed up in this?' said Amy.

'We wanted to be popular, remember?' said Karen, wondering where the popularity was.

The girls sat there not speaking for a minute, just drinking their drinks. Then Amy put her glass down.

'What if we told the police?' she said.

'You can't be serious!' said Karen.

'I think I am,' said Amy. 'Listen, the worst that would happen is Ryan's plans are stopped and he goes to jail. If we are part of those plans, we go to jail too! But if we stop him, they may let us off.'

'Yeah but then what happens when Ryan is released. He'll come for us both!' said Karen.

'Karen, he's been coming for me for the last two years! I've been assaulted in so many ways and so many times I've lost count!' said Amy.

Karen put her arm round her friend. 'I know and I'm worried it'll happen again.'

Amy turned to face Karen. 'Are you worried for me or for you?' she asked.

'To be honest, both!' said Karen. 'Look, we've been mates a lot longer that Ryan's been on the scene and we will be after he's gone.'

'Let's stick together and do this,' said Amy. 'Let's look out for each other!'

'Okay,' said Karen, sounding a little reluctant, but at the same time realising her friend was right.

Once they'd finished their drinks. They left the cafe and walked to the end of the street. They turned right and walked about three blocks until they came to a large roundabout with a pedestrian underpass beneath it. They walked through and as they came up the other side the County Police Station was right in front of them.

'You sure you want to do this?' said Karen.

'Yeah, I'm sure,' said Amy.

The two of them walked through the door and up to the front desk.

'How can I help you?' asked the police officer from behind the counter.

'We need to talk to someone,' said Amy. 'There's going to be a terror attack on Parliament tomorrow!'

The officer paused for a moment, taking in what they'd said.

'Right, you two, wait there a moment,' she said turning to speak to her sergeant.

Moments later a door to their right opened and the officer walked through.

'Come with me, please,' she said.

She took Amy and Karen through to an interview room.

Explaining that they weren't under arrest or being charged with anything, she cautioned them.

'Why are you doing that?' asked Karen.

'So the evidence you give us can be used in court when we catch whoever is planning this,' replied the officer.

Moments later they were joined by a high-ranking detective.

'Hi girls, I'm DCI Sunderland. Can you please tell me everything you know?'

Amy and Karen took it in turns to share what they knew about Ryan's plan. They told the police about the bombs and how they worked. They told them about the planned attack in the US. Amy also told them about the abuse she'd experienced over the last few years. She lifted her shirt to show her tummy to the officers. It was covered in bruises and cuts.

'Okay,' said DCI Sunderland, 'we'll get a medical officer to take a proper look at you after this interview, if that's okay?'

'Yes, of course,' said Amy, feeling relieved someone with the power to do something finally knew.

At the end of the interview, Amy and Karen were told to wait until their parents could get there. Some forty minutes later Amy's mum arrived. She and Amy were taken to see the medical officer. Amy and her mum entered the examination room. The M.O. asked Amy to take her clothes off. As she did her mother started to cry. She had no idea her daughter was so badly injured. Amy had been very careful to hide this out of fear. Once the M.O. was finished, she reassured Amy and her mum that she would fully heal from the physical scars, but recommended some counselling support for Amy.

The police had contacted MI5, who had dispatched an officer to interview the girls. As they finished with the medical examination, the officer arrived at the station.

'Good evening. I'm Agent Murphy, MI5,' he said.

'Ah, yes we've been expecting you,' said the officer on the front desk.

Agent Murphy was taken through to an interview room where the girls were sitting with their mums.

'Hello, I'm Agent Murphy, MI5,' he said. The girls introduced themselves.

Amy's mother then asked, 'Are these two in trouble?'

'That depends, ma'am,' said Agent Murphy.

'On what?' asked Karen's mum.

'On how much they help us in the next twenty-four hours.'

'But they've told you what they know,' said Amy's mum.

'Yes, they have,' said Agent Murphy, 'but the cold fact is your daughter has been under MI5 surveillance for months as a suspected terror cell member. She's been involved in the planning of an attack she's only now telling us about.'

'Oh,' said Amy's mother, backing down somewhat.

'Look,' said Agent Murphy, 'they've done the right thing coming forward. What we need now is for them to help us stop the attack happening. If they want to clear their names, they don't have a choice in this.'

'Mum, we want to help. We don't want to be part of this,' said Amy.

'Very well,' said Agent Murphy, 'then this is what we need you to do...'

Chapter 20

The Atlantic Manoeuvre

The van pulled into Thames House and Martin, Riley, Casey and Alex wasted no time getting out and going into the building. Martin had radioed ahead and Section Chief Roberts was already waiting with Sir Richard Marsden. As they came into the briefing room, James from the CIA joined them.

'Take a seat, everyone,' said Director General Marsden.

'Okay, Riley,' said Section Chief Roberts, 'please can you share your latest intel with us.'

Riley cleared her throat with a little cough before starting.

'Yes, ma'am,' she said. 'I attended the London FWO cell meeting at 3.30 p.m. this afternoon. Everything I'm about to share with you has been recorded using my phone.'

'We're having the data transferred now, ma'am,' interjected Martin. He smiled at Riley, beckoning her to continue.

'At this meeting, the London cell revealed they plan to enter Parliament at 3.00 p.m. tomorrow and collect their bomb packages.'

'What do you mean, "collect" them?' asked Sir Richard.

'Apparently, they're already on site, sir,' said Riley, 'it would appear Parliament has a security breach.'

'My God,' replied Sir Richard, 'is the PM or the Cabinet at risk?'

'Not that I'm aware of, sir,' replied Riley. 'The cell leadership didn't mention them at any point. They did say they plan to assemble the bomb in the House of Commons and once the timer is set it will take one minute to detonate.'

'The problem we have,' said Martin, 'is we don't know where the breach is, so searching the building tonight could tip them off. Also, we need to be able to arrest the suspects on site with the bomb equipment.'

'Agreed,' said Sir Richard.

Riley interrupted, 'There is more, sir.'

'Please continue,' said Sir Richard.

'The cell leader, Ryan Peters, also revealed a major security breach in the US.'

James sat forward in his chair at this point and asked, 'What security breach?'

'Apparently someone in our Capitol Police has leaked the entire FBI plan. They've changed their target as a result and may have inside help to access the building. The only good news is they don't know the FBI plans to replace members of Congress with agents.'

'Director General,' said James, 'this is a serious problem. If we inform our Security Services, we risk the cell changing plans again with no way to find out what they are.'

'Do you know the details of the new target?' said Sir Richard.

'Yes, sir,' said Riley, 'they plan to destroy the White House at 10.00 a.m. DC time tomorrow.'

'The same time the London cell attacks Westminster,' said Alex, who had sat quietly listening until now.

'We need to be back in the US,' said Casey, looking at James.

'I agree with you, young lady,' said Sir Richard.

'But sir, what about Parliament?' asked Section Chief Roberts.

'There isn't anything more Riley can do here,' said Sir Richard. 'We have good intel and our government is out of danger. However, the Americans aren't in the same position. Martin is it possible to get these three and James back to DC by 9.00 a.m. local time?'

'No, sir, not on a commercial flight,' replied Martin.

'What about a military aircraft?' asked the Director General.

'I'll look into it immediately, sir,' said Martin, getting up from the table.

'Is there anything else you can tell us?' asked Section

Chief Roberts.

'Only one thing,' said Riley. 'This isn't a national security issue, but you'll have a film from my phone of Ryan Peters trying to attack a girl called Amy in the changing rooms at the school. She is one of his cell members but from what we've learnt this week, he's assaulted her on several occasions. I'd be grateful if you'd add that to the list of charges against him,' she said.

'Absolutely,' said Section Chief Roberts.

'Thank you, ma'am,' said Riley.

Martin returned to the room. 'I've spoken to the Ministry of Defence and they're arranging a jet to take the four of you from RAF Northolt to Andrews Airforce Base. From there a helicopter will take you straight to the White House.'

'Can a small jet plane get that far quickly enough?' asked Sir Richard.

'It can if it refuels on the HMS Queen Elizabeth currently on manoeuvres in the Atlantic Ocean,' replied Martin.

'Very well,' said Sir Richard. 'What time do they need to leave?'

'Now, sir,' said Martin. 'I've sent officers to their hotel to collect their belongings and take them to RAF Northolt.'

'Very well,' said Sir Richard, standing to his feet. 'Riley, Casey, Alex, James thank you all for your service to Her Majesty's Government. I wish you Godspeed and success in saving your own government.'

'Thank you, sir,' they each replied as they shook his hand on the way out of the briefing room.

'Sir, there is one more thing,' said Martin. 'Two girls from the school we've been watching have just walked into a police station and told the desk about the attack.'

'What are their names?' asked Riley.

'Amy and Karen,' replied Martin.

'Fantastic,' said Riley.

'Martin, I want you down there to interview them as soon as possible,' said Sir Richard.

'It's already taken care of, sir,' replied Martin. 'Agent

Murphy is there now.'

As they made their way through Thames House, Casey asked, 'Martin, will someone get our NASA flight suits to the Airforce Base?'

'Yes, Casey, it's already been taken care of,' replied Martin.

'That's good,' said Alex, 'I have a weird feeling we are gonna need them!'

'Me too,' said Riley.

Speed was now of the essence. So, getting to RAF Northolt involved going to the roof of Thames House and boarding a helicopter.

'It's the only way you'll get past all that London traffic at this time of day,' said Martin.

'Are you coming with us?' asked Riley.

'No,' replied Martin, 'this is where I leave you as I have to be part of the operation here now. Besides I need to speak to Agent Murphy and find out what Amy and Karen have told him!'

'Thanks for everything,' said Alex shaking Martin by the hand.

Riley was a lot less formal and gave Martin a hug. So did Casey, before they both boarded the helicopter. Martin watched from the edge of the helipad as they lifted off and turned to fly north and west towards the airbase.

They were met at RAF Northolt by Squadron Leader Benson.

'Good evening, please follow me,' he said. 'Your jet is waiting to take you to Andrews. There was no time for niceties. This was now a military operation until they reached Washington. The four of them followed the Squadron Leader as he hurried them through the base and out onto the runway. There, prepped and ready, was a small jet plane. The pilot was already on board, as were their personal belongings and, more importantly, their NASA flight suits. Riley and the others boarded the jet and strapped into the seats. Squadron Leader Benson had a quick word with the pilot before wishing them a safe flight. As soon as he'd disembarked, the jet doors were sealed and they taxied for take-off.

'Prepare yourselves,' said the pilot. 'This will be a faster take-off than you're used to. We should reach the aircraft carrier in approximately four hours,' he added.

He wasn't wrong, Riley's stomach twisted and turned as the jet shot into the air. Once it levelled out, she began to feel like herself again.

'You okay?' asked James looking a Riley's contorted expression.

'Yeah, I am now we're up,' she said.

'We need to discuss what we are going to do when we reach the Andrews Airbase,' said James.

'I've been thinking about that,' said Riley.

'Go on,' said Alex.

'Well I think the fastest way to get to the White House would be to use the NASA flight suits,' said Riley.

'How do they work?' asked James, who'd not seen them train in the suits.

'They're a highly classified anti-gravity suit,' said Casey. 'Ours are fitted with rocket boosters. Riley's isn't, as she can create her own energy pulse.'

'They sound incredible,' said James, sounding slightly in awe of the suits.

'Yeah, they are pretty cool,' said Alex.

'So, what will you do when you get to the White House?' asked James.

'We will locate Cannons and the cell and stop them,' said Riley.

'The problem you have is you don't know how they plan to get the bomb into the White House, if indeed they can,' said James.

'True,' said Alex, 'the one advantage we do have is they don't know we're coming or that anyone from the Security Services is aware they have changed their plans.'

'I hope you three know what you're doing,' said James. 'A lot is riding on this.'

'No pressure then!' said Casey.

Alex and Casey made the most of the four hours on the flight to HMS Queen Elizabeth by checking everything on the NASA flight suits was in working order. They also found the plane's small galley and made something to eat.

'Have you ever been on an aircraft carrier?' Casey asked James.

'No, this will be a first for me,' he replied.

'I've only been on the USS Intrepid in New York,' said Alex.

'Let me guess,' said Casey, 'that's the Air and Space Museum, isn't it?'

'Yup,' replied Alex, with a grin on his face.

'You're such an adorable geek,' said Riley.

'Why thank you,' said Alex.

Casey raised her eyebrows at Riley's choice of adjective, but said nothing.

'We're on final approach,' said the pilot. 'Time to strap in.'

Everyone made themselves comfortable and put on their seatbelts.

'This will be a sudden stop as the runway isn't long on a ship,' said the pilot.

Everyone braced themselves; they could feel the aircraft losing altitude but it was dark outside and out at sea there were no lights. Suddenly the jet touched down and there was a horrendous noise as the flaps flew open and the engines went into full reverse. Finally, the jet came to an abrupt halt at the end of the aircraft carrier's runway. The jolt made all of them appreciate the seat belts they were wearing!

As the engines powered down, the door opened and a Royal Navy Officer boarded the jet.

'Good evening everyone. My name is Commander Gary Taylor and I'm First Officer on HMS Queen Elizabeth. Welcome aboard,' he said.

'Thank you, sir,' replied Alex.

'I appreciate you folks are in a hurry so we will have you refuelled and in the air in approximately twenty minutes,' said the Commander.

'That's much appreciated,' said James.

'Sir,' said Alex, 'while we wait may I make a request?'

'By all means,' said Commander Taylor.

'Could we step onto the flight deck for a few minutes?' asked Alex.

'Not something we'd normally do, but this whole situation isn't normal so yes, why not?' replied the Commander.

'Thank you so much,' said Alex. He turned to Riley and Casey. 'Coming, you two?'

'I'll stay put if that's okay,' said Casey, but Riley was also up on her feet and replied, 'Yes, count me in.'

Commander Taylor led them down onto the flight deck. It was dark but they could see the moonlight twinkling on the sea. He walked them across the runway to get a view of the ship and the ocean. They could smell a mix of salty sea air and aviation fuel. Without realising she was doing it, Riley took hold of Alex's hand. He didn't seem to mind.

'This must be a dream come true for you,' she said to him.

'Just a bit,' he replied.

Alex asked the Commander a few geeky questions about the ship and the aircraft it carried. He was careful to avoid questions about the ship's arsenal as he was aware that would be classified.

After a few minutes, the Commander suggested they return to their jet and get ready for departure.

'Thank you for this opportunity, sir,' said Alex.

'Yes, thank you,' added Riley.

'Not a problem,' said Commander Taylor, 'and you two make a cute couple, if you don't mind me saying.'

Riley and Alex looked at each other, both turning red. Riley realised she was still holding Alex's hand, so let go quickly. Neither of them replied to Commander Taylor, but just walked in an awkward silence back to the jet. Neither of them had been expecting that manoeuvre in the Atlantic!

Once on board, the Commander said goodbye and the door was sealed. The pilot told them to buckle up ready for take-off.

Chapter 21

Flight

The jet turned on the aircraft carrier's runway and positioned itself for take-off.

'Ready, everyone,' said the pilot as he pushed the throttle and the jet began to move.

Riley and the others were held firmly in their seats with the sheer force at which the jet was moving. The noise was deafening as they launched into the night sky and continued the journey westwards towards the United States.

'We should be at Andrews Airforce Base around 3.30 a.m. local time as we gain five hours with the time difference,' said the pilot.

'Thanks,' replied James.

'Do you want me to radio ahead and let anyone know you're coming?' asked the pilot.

'Give us a minute,' said James. He turned to the others. 'Guys, if we announce our arrival, they'll know something is up and this may alert the FWO.'

'Didn't you say Ryan had said the breach came from the Capitol Police?' Alex asked Riley.

'Yes, I did,' she replied.

'So, on that basis we should be safe asking Director Andrews to meet us at the airbase,' said Alex.

'Why would we do that?' asked Casey.

'Several reasons,' said Riley. 'Firstly, he's our line manager, secondly, he's the head of Operation Legion and finally if we are changing our mission he needs to know.'

'Yes, but only him!' added Alex.

'Agreed,' said James.

James went through to the cockpit and told the pilot to send a message via Andrews Airbase to the Director of the Secret Service. When he returned to his seat the others were all sat very quiet.

'You all okay?' he asked.

'Yes, thanks,' said Casey. The others didn't reply. James and Casey looked at Alex and Riley. They both seemed miles away, as if their minds were elsewhere.

'Hey, you two!' shouted Casey. 'Are you still with us?'

'Oh yeah, sorry,' said Riley.

'Yeah, fine,' said Alex.

'What's going on?' said Casey, suspiciously.

'Nothing,' said Riley, giving Alex a quick sideways look.

She, like him, had been thinking about Commander Taylor's comment on the flight deck of HMS Queen Elizabeth.

'We're fine,' said Alex, 'just a little tired, that's all.'

'Well why don't we try and get a couple of hours rest before we land,' suggested James.

He dimmed the cabin lights and handed round some blankets. Everyone settled down to try and sleep. Riley sat in her chair holding her blanket, knowing sleep wasn't likely as she had too much going on in her mind.

The flight seemed to drag on for Riley, while the others slept. She had been thinking a lot about Amy and Karen. She was pleased they'd decided to do the right thing. She was also pleased she'd told Section Chief Roberts what Ryan had done to Amy. But, for most of the flight, Riley's thoughts had been about home. She'd not seen her brother and sister or her mum in months. She'd not spoken to them in over a week. The most frustrating thing about all this was not being able to tell her mum. She'd thought about asking for permission to speak to her mum, but she realised that if her mum knew it wouldn't help. Her mum would probably stop her from taking part in all this, deeming it too dangerous.

Director Andrews arrived at the security gates at the airbase.

'Can I see some identification please, sir?' said the guard. As the guard looked at the I.D. he said, 'Ah, Director Andrews, the base Commander is expecting you.'

'Okay guys, time to buckle up. We are on final approach to Andrews Airforce Base,' said the pilot.

Riley nudged the others awake and told them to buckle up as the plane started its final decent towards the runway. The plane came into land. This was a much softer landing than the one on the aircraft carrier.

The jet taxied to a nearby hangar where they all disembarked. Waiting for them in the hangar was Director Andrews.

'Hello, sir,' said Riley, 'we need to talk.'

'What's going on, Riley? Why are you here when your assignment is in London?'

'Sir, there's been a major security breach,' said Riley. 'The FWO know our plans for the Capitol, sir,' she said. 'As a result, they've changed their target and will bomb the White House at 10.00 a.m. today!'

'Right,' said Director Andrews, 'come with me.'

They followed him as he led them to the Base Commander's office. On arrival they were met by Colonel Stewart.

'Good morning, Colonel,' said Director Andrews. 'Thank you for allowing us to meet on your base this morning.'

'Not a problem,' replied the Colonel, 'let me know if there's anything you need.' With that he left his office for James, the Director and the three teenagers to meet.

'Riley, do you know any of the details of this new attack?' asked Director Andrews.

'Other than the time and target, no, sir,' she replied.

'What do you propose we do, sir?' asked Alex.

'This is a difficult situation,' said the Director. 'If we try to get more intelligence, we run the risk of giving away details of what we currently know.'

'Can I make a suggestion?' said Riley.

'Of course,' replied the Director.

'Let the FBI and Capitol Police carry on as planned. I presume all the agents are currently on their way to the Capitol dressed as Congressmen and women?'

'They should be by now,' said the Director.

'What next, though?' asked Casey.

'Well,' said Riley, 'I suggest we get the three of us to the White House. I have my suspicions about how they'll attack.'

'What are you thinking?' asked James.

'I'm thinking this is a last-minute change. They've had no time to prepare to infiltrate the White House so they'll take the fastest most direct approach,' said Riley.

'You think they're going to attack from the air, don't you?' said Alex.

'Yeah, I do,' said Riley, 'which is why you need us there with our anti-gravity flight suits.'

'But surely the White House can defend an air attack,' said Casey.

'Yes, they can,' said Director Andrews, 'unless that defence is disabled or destroyed. Very well, let's get you to the White House.'

Director Andrews asked Colonel Stewart to provide a helicopter to get them to the White House as quickly as possible. The Colonel, being the consummate professional that he was, had anticipated such a request and had the helicopter ready with a pilot waiting.

'If you don't mind, sir, can I take your car and drive to Langley?' said James. 'I should really report back in.'

'Yes, by all means,' said Director Andrews.

The remaining four of them left the Colonel's office and headed to the helicopter. The Colonel had made sure their belongings had been moved from the jet to the helicopter. This included their NASA flight suits. Once again, they took to the skies, this time over more familiar ground. The flight from Andrews to the White House didn't take too long, especially compared with the one they'd just done across the Atlantic Ocean.

Once the helicopter had touched down on the South Lawn of the White House, Director Andrews, Riley, Casey and Alex made their way to the office of the White House Chief of Staff.

'Good morning, Grace,' said Director Andrews, 'may we have a word?' They made their way in and sat down.

'What's going on, Jack? I though these three were on assignment in London with MI5,' said Grace.

'There's been a change of plan,' said Director Andrews. He then briefed Grace on the current threat which was now less than two hours away.

'We need to inform POTUS immediately,' said Grace, 'Jack, Riley, followed me please.' Grace got up from her desk as Director Andrews and Riley stood up.

'You two wait here, please,' said Jack to Alex and Casey.

'Yes, sir,' They both replied.

Riley followed Grace and Jack through the West Wing and into the Oval Office once more.

'Sir,' said Grace, 'sorry to disturb you but I have Director Andrews here with an urgent update.'

'Come in, Jack, Riley. Take a seat please,' said the President.

'Thank you, Mr President,' replied Jack.

Over the next ten minutes, Riley and Jack updated the President on the mission with MI5 and the resulting change of FWO plans in Washington.

'And you surmise the threat to the White House is an air attack?' said the President.

'Yes, sir, it's Riley's theory, but I have to agree it is the most likely outcome,' said Jack.

'Very well,' said the President, 'and Riley you want to attempt to stop it using the NASA suits and your flying skills?'

'Yes, sir, if for some reason the White House defences don't stop them, we will be ready.'

'This is exceptionally brave of you,' said the President, 'but it's a quality I've come to admire in you and your friends. Very well, Jack give Riley and her team access to the roof and then join me in the Presidential Emergency Operations Centre.'

'Yes, Mr President,' said Jack.

Chapter 22

The Terror of Two Cities

The Director of the Secret Service led Riley back to Grace's office. Waiting there were Alex and Casey.

'What's going on, Riley?' said Casey.

'We are going to defend the White House,' replied Riley.

'Okay, you three,' said Jack, 'get your NASA suits and follow me.'

Riley, Casey and Alex picked up their flight packs and followed Director Andrews up several flights of stairs, past the control room to the roof of the building. There they found a number of Secret Service agents positioned to watch for any kind of attack.

'The President wants me in the PEOC,' said Director Andrews, 'so I'm going to leave you three here. I want you to take whatever action you see fit to protect the White House.'

'Yes, sir,' replied Riley.

Riley, Casey and Alex unpacked their NASA flight packs and put the suits on. Riley noticed her pack had been fitted with thrusters like Casey and Alex's suits. *I wonder why they've added those to my suit?* she thought to herself as she could use her energy pulse to fly. Once they were kitted up, Riley asked Alex to help her spin invisible. As she finished turning around and around her brain burn began and he caught her in his arms to stop her falling. Being held by him was a nice feeling, but not one she'd be sharing with anyone right now.

In London there was less than an hour until the attack on Westminster was due to take place. MI5 had kitted Amy and Karen out with body armour under their clothes to protect them in case of a blast. They had then been released and allowed to rejoin Ryan and his cell ready for the attack.

Riley, Casey and Alex sat down on the White House roof and looked around. There was a good view of Washington from where they were. They could see clearly in all directions.

'What if I've got this wrong?' said Riley.

'Don't start doubting yourself,' said Casey, 'it won't do you any good.'

'Also, didn't the Director back you in the Oval Office?' asked Alex.

'Yeah he did,' said Riley.

'Well then,' said Alex, 'if he thinks your theory is the most likely outcome, then we all should.'

'I guess so,' said Riley.

Section Chief Roberts, Martin and their MI5 team had been in position for several hours now. The Prime Minister had ordered a COBRA meeting which had briefed senior ministers and given Sir Richard a chance to share MI5's plans. Section Chief Roberts was now watching an approaching school group as they entered the parliament building for their afternoon tour.

'Agent Shepherd, I have just seen Amy and Karen enter Westminster with a group of about eight others. There were several adults, none of whom I can confirm the identity of,' she said.

'Very well, ma'am, we are in position in the Commons Chamber,' replied Martin.

One of the Secret Service agents on the roof came over to where Riley and co were sitting. 'I thought there were three of you up here,' he said to Casey and Alex.

'There are,' replied Casey. Riley tapped the agent on the shoulder. He spun around, but saw no-one.

'What the...?' he said.

'She's invisible,' replied Casey.

'Oh, wow,' said the agent.

Just then another agent walked over.

'Heads up, everyone, we have an unidentified aircraft on

approach,' she said.

Alex was still sitting down and jumped to his feet.

'Hand me some binoculars,' said Riley. Casey handed her some and she took a look.

'It looks like a modified helicopter,' she said.

'Modified how?' said Alex, looking through the binoculars. 'You're right, it's got heavy weapons attached.'

'Positions, everyone,' said the female agent.

Riley looked as if she was preparing to leave.

'What are you doing?' asked Casey.

'Getting up in the air,' said Riley, 'there's nothing I can do standing on this roof!'

Amy and Karen followed the others as they made their way through the parliament building towards the House of Commons. Unbeknown to them, the cell were being watched by MI5. They stopped just before reaching the Commons Chamber and opened a door to what appeared to be a small meeting room.

'Excuse me,' said the tour guide with them, 'you can't go in there!'

'Shut up,' replied Ryan, grabbing the tour guide and gagging her. Others came over and helped tie her to a chair.

As Amy entered the room, she saw the packs they had been told so much about. Some of the group had helped keep them hidden for weeks.

'Take one of these each,' said Ryan from beneath a disguise he was wearing to make him appear as an elderly man. Amy looked worried as she picked up a pack.

'Don't look so worried, babe,' said Ryan grabbing her arm and pulling her towards him. Karen wasted no time grabbing Amy and pulling her away from him. Fortunately, he didn't react, clearly more focussed on his mission. He told the group to get ready to move on.

Back in DC, the helicopter was getting closer to the White House. Before Casey and Alex could say anything, Riley had launched into the air using her energy pulse to lift off from the roof. They watched as she soared high into the sky above them. Then the unthinkable happened! The helicopter launched a missile towards the roof of the White House! Alex and Casey watched in disbelief as Riley flew into the missile's path. Activating her suit's thrusters, Riley was able to put her hand out and release an energy pulse towards the missile. To the amazement of Alex and Casey, who were the only ones seeing this, the missile slowed in mid-air. Riley then flew towards it, grabbed it and lowered it safely to the ground. The Secret Service agents and the people in the helicopter couldn't believe their eyes as they saw the missile slow to a halt in mid-air then gently descend to the ground without exploding.

Ryan led Amy and the others towards the Commons Chamber.

'You know what to do inside,' he said. 'Be quick, no mucking about. We get one shot at this and if we succeed it will be a great victory!'

As they entered the chamber it appeared to be empty. They made their way to the table in the centre of the chamber where the Prime Minister stood to address the House. Putting their bags down, they pulled out their USB cables ready to connect the packs.

Riley shot back into the air coming in to land near her friends on the roof.

'I'm gonna need your help,' she said. 'A missile is one thing but an entire helicopter will take all of us.'

Alex and Casey looked at her with stunned faces.

'We don't have super powers, you know!' said Casey.

'I know,' said Riley, 'but you can fly and create a distraction, while I find a way to ground that helicopter!'

'Come on,' said Ryan, 'we ain't got all day!'

Some of the teenagers had connected their packs to the ones either side of them. Amy was taking her time.

'What the hell you doing, Amy? Come on!' yelled Ryan.

He came around the table and grabbed the cable from her to fit it himself. Once he'd done it, he turned to her and slapped her in the face.

'You're a stupid cow, you know that!' he said.

'Leave her alone,' said Karen, getting in between the two of them.

Riley, Casey and Alex took off from the White House roof and flew towards the helicopter.

'Be careful, you two,' said Riley. 'They can see you!'

Sure enough, the terrorists on the helicopter had spotted Alex and Casey and were trying to shoot them down. But their NASA flight suits were too fast and they ran rings round the cell members. Secret Service agents had opened fire on the helicopter which was also keeping the cell members on board busy.

Meanwhile Riley had flown up underneath the helicopter and was holding on to its undercarriage. She noticed a fuel control panel above her head and pulled it open. Turning the lever inside, she opened the value and fuel started to leak from the helicopter.

Chris Cannons shouted from the cockpit, 'We're losing fuel, we're not gonna make it over the White House!'

The helicopter started to lose power. Then suddenly the engines stalled and the rotor blades began to slow down.

'We're going down!' shouted Cannons as the helicopter dived towards the White House lawn.

As it crashed on the grass, Riley, Casey and Alex flew down to see if its occupants were alive. Secret Service agents came running onto the lawn as the three teenagers landed, and surrounded the downed helicopter. With guns out pointing at the doors, they advanced towards the helicopter.

'Careful,' said Alex, 'there's aviation fuel everywhere.'

'Hold your fire,' shouted one of the Secret Service agents. He'd heard Alex and realised a spark could blow the lot.

Finally, the last cable was ready to go in.

'As soon as this one's in,' said Ryan, 'run!'

Just as he was about to place it, MI5 officers appeared from behind many of the back benches of the House. They'd concealed themselves there before the terrorist cell arrived.

'Hold it right there!' said Martin, pointing a gun at Ryan. Ryan, still holding the cable, pushed it into the socket, activating the bomb.

'Run! he shouted, and as Ryan started to run towards the door Martin shot him in the leg, causing him to fall to the floor. The teenagers screamed and froze to the spot, putting their hands up.

'The bomb!' shouted Amy, in a terrified voice.

Riley advanced towards the helicopter and opened the door. There were still people alive inside. Casey, Alex and the other agents rushed forward to pull people from the crashed helicopter. Riley recognised kids from the school and bookstore. As they pulled them from the wreckage, there was lots of crying and screaming as many of the teenagers had broken limbs. One of the girls Casey pulled from the helicopter had nearly passed out with shock. She'd lost an arm in the crash and was covered in blood.

Before she fainted, she turned to Casey and said, 'Bomb!'

Casey shouted, 'Get back everyone! Now! There's a bomb on board.'

Everyone ran in different directions away from the crashed helicopter. Some were carrying, or dragging teenagers with them. As they cleared the immediate area, Riley stepped forward. Alex and Casey watched as the helicopter exploded in an enormous ball of fire and fuel.

'Riley!' screamed Casey. But Riley wasn't there. She'd fired her flight suit thrusters and was in the air over the explosion. From there she raised her hand and sent a continuous energy pulse at the helicopter. It pushed the flames from the explosion back. She kept firing the pulse until the fire went out. However, the energy pulse had drained her, the shock had made her visible again and she was now falling from the sky. Alex saw this and was already in the air racing towards her. He caught her in his arms just metres above the wreckage. Turning mid-air, he flew towards Casey and landed, still carrying Riley.

Martin quickly gave orders for the remaining cell members to be taken out and arrested, Karen and Amy included.

'Get the bomb squad in here now!' He shouted. Fortunately, due to Riley's intel, the bomb squad were already on site and entered as soon as the terrorists were led out.

'It's on a sixty second timer, guys,' said Martin as he followed his team out of the chamber.

Bomb Squad officers ran to the table to see what they were dealing with.

'We need to find the trigger,' said one of them unzipping the base of each bag.

'Here,' said another, pointing at a pack with a computer unit in. They worked fast and managed to neutralise the bomb just seconds before detonation.

Chapter 23

The Needle in the Haystack

Alex knelt on the ground with Riley still in his arms. Casey ran towards them and stopped by falling to her knees opposite Alex. Riley coughed and opened her eyes.

'Are you okay?' asked Alex.

'Yeah, thanks to you,' she said, pulling him towards her and kissing him.

'I knew it!' said Casey smiling, 'I knew you two had a thing.'

'This isn't a thing,' said Alex, defensively.

'Oh, I think it is!' said Riley kissing him again. The girls started laughing. Alex smiled.

'Come on, let's get you checked out,' he said, by way of changing the conversation.

As the three of them stood up, they could see the aftermath of the failed attack. Secret Service agents had started accompanying teenagers into the backs of ambulances which were now arriving on the lawn. A fire truck pulled up next to the wreckage. Director Andrews came across the grass from the East Wing of the White House.

'Hey you three, you all okay?' he asked.

'Yeah we're okay, sir,' said Alex.

'You did it,' said Jack. 'I've just heard from London. Martin's team stopped the Westminster bombers, with the help of Amy and Karen.'

'That's fantastic,' said Riley.

'What was fantastic,' said Jack, 'was the way you stopped that missile, brought down a helicopter and then controlled an explosion so only one person was killed.'

'Oh my God, who, sir?' said Riley.

'Chris Cannons. He was piloting the helicopter and we couldn't pull him clear before the explosion,' said the

Director.

'What about Ryan Peters in London, sir? asked Riley.

'Agent Shepherd shot him in the leg,' said Director Andrews, 'but he'll recover in time to stand trial.'

In London, MI5 officers had started to close off parts of Westminster for their forensic team to begin work. Amy and Karen had told Martin about the tour guide tied up in the side room. An officer had gone to assist her and get a statement. Martin's team was now transporting Amy and Karen and the other members of the terrorist cell to Thames House for interrogation.

As they stood talking on the lawn with emergency crews all around them, two special agents came running towards them from the White House. As they arrived, the female agent spoke.

'Sir, it's not over!' she said.

'What do you mean?' asked Director Andrews.

'There's another bomb!' replied the Special Agent.

'Where?' asked Riley.

'At the Capitol,' she replied.

'I thought the intelligence said they'd changed from the Capitol to the White House,' said Alex.

'It had,' said the Special Agent, 'and it was correct intel as far as we knew.' She glanced across at the crashed helicopter. 'But,' she continued, 'MI5 just contacted us. One of the kids they arrested has been gloating, saying we've stopped nothing.'

'What do we know?' asked the Director.

'Only that it's a lone bomber in the crowd gathered for the annual concert,' said the special agent.

Director Andrews turned to Riley. 'Can you turn invisible again?' he said.

'I can try,' she said, still feeling drained from containing the helicopter explosion.

'What do you want her to do, sir?' asked Alex, sounding concerned.

145

'I don't want to startle the crowds or alert the bomber,' he said, 'so if Riley can fly over the event and identify the bomber from the air, we can move in to his, or her, location and stop them.'

'Very well, sir,' said Riley, stepping away from them.

'You sure you've got the strength for this?' asked Casey.

'I hope so,' said Riley as she raised her arms and started to spin.

Suddenly she felt her brain burning. Both Alex and Casey ran to grab her and stop her falling. As the pain died down Riley thanked her friends.

'I'll radio in as soon as I spot something,' she said, and with that she shot into the air and flew towards the Mall.

Turning left she slingshot her way round the Washington Monument and headed down the Mall towards the Capitol Building. There were literally thousands of people below her, all celebrating the fourth of July. As she got closer to the Capitol the crowds became dense. How was she meant to spot one suspicious-looking person amongst so many? It would be like trying to find a needle in a haystack! She reported in on her headset radio.

'Okay, Riley,' said Alex, 'I have a hunch our suspect will be one of the teenagers from the Jefferson Memorial High School.'

'Okay, I'll keep looking,' replied Riley.

Back at the White House, Casey had raised a question. 'How did they get a bomb past the event security?' she said.

'Possibly our Capitol Police leak,' said Alex.

'If we can capture this bomber,' said the Director, 'they may provide some answers.'

Riley reduced her altitude so she was closer to the crowd. It allowed her to get a closer look at people. But who was she looking for? Her mind started to picture the faces of those they'd rescued from the downed helicopter. Who was missing from that group? Who could it be? Her flight path had her zigzagging north and south across the Mall, edging ever closer to the Capitol and the front of the crowd. She'd remembered faces, mainly the boys from 11R. So, who had she missed?

As Riley flew over the heads of the crowd, she saw her suspect. Standing there looking just the same as those around her was Wendy, the girl from 11R, the girl from that first gathering in the bathroom at Jefferson Memorial High. But where was the bomb? Riley slowed her approach and hovered in the air around six metres above Wendy. She looked around to see if there was anything suspicious. Riley was about to give up and move on when she noticed Wendy bend down and pull a bag from under her chair.

Taking a USB cable from her pocket she plugged one end into the base of the bag. Riley watched wondering what she'd do next. The terrorists had planned to use multiple bags to create a bomb of many parts, but Wendy was alone. Where would the other end of the cable go? Then Riley saw it. Wendy had some sort of package strapped to her. Her jacket was hiding most of it. Riley could see she was looking where to place the cable. *If she gets that in place,* thought Riley, *it could activate the bomb!*

There was no time to call it in. Riley dived through the air towards Wendy, landing in front of her. Riley threw her arms around Wendy and shot back into the air, taking the teenager and the bomb with her. Wendy let out an almighty scream as she flew up into the air. Those around had no idea what was happening as Riley's electrical field had cloaked Wendy from their view.

Riley flew full pelt down the Mall towards the Lincoln Memorial. She had to get Wendy clear of the crowds. As they passed the giant needle of the Washington Monument, Wendy started to try and struggle free. She twisted and turned in Riley's arms. Wendy couldn't be sure but had a feeling someone was carrying her. As they passed the Washington Monument, Alex and Casey saw them fly past from the south lawn of the White House. They told Director Andrews, who immediately ordered agents to head to the Lincoln Memorial.

Wendy was fighting Riley in mid-air now. Trying to reach the cable to plug it into her chest pack. Alex could see the mid-air battle between the girls.

'Sir, we have to help her. If she is carrying a bomb it could kill Riley,' he said.

'Very well,' said Director Andrews. He knew full well if the thousands of people on the Mall saw two teenagers in anti-gravity flight suits there would be questions to answer. But lives were at stake so he ordered Alex and Casey to engage.

They launched together flying high into the air before changing course towards the Mall. Riley and Wendy were about half way between the Washington Monument and Lincoln Memorial. The others took just seconds to reach them. Alex and Casey grabbed each of Wendy's arms pulling them away from her body. Riley was finally able to take one hand off Wendy, without the fear of dropping her. It meant she could at last remove the USB cable from the two-piece bomb.

With the threat neutralised, they brought Wendy down to the ground. As they did, a number of FBI and Secret Service agents pulled up in cars with lights and sirens going, then an ambulance and fire truck appeared, clearly there in case things had gone badly. Agents came running towards them with guns drawn. Alex stood up with his hands up.

'It's okay,' he said, 'it's under control.'

He purposely didn't use the word 'bomb' as there were members of the public within earshot. Agents moved in and took over from Riley, Alex and Casey. They removed Wendy's bag and the device she was wearing. She was led away by the FBI in handcuffs to a waiting vehicle which was designed for prisoner transport.

Director Andrews pulled up in a Secret Service 4x4. Getting out, he walked across to speak to the three of them.

Chapter 24

The Big Question

'I want you three in an ambulance,' said Director Andrews. 'Once you've been checked out at Walter Reed Hospital, I'll make arrangements for your debriefing.'

'Yes, sir,' they all replied.

Riley was still very wobbly after containing the explosion at the White House. Carrying Wendy so far hadn't helped. Alex had hold of her and wasn't letting go. Casey went to Riley's free arm and placed it round her shoulder. Then the three of them made their way slowly across the grass to the nearby ambulance. Casey and Alex helped Riley up the steps. Once inside she made herself visible again. A paramedic, slightly stunned by this, took over and got her onto the bed. All three of them were still in their NASA flight gear. Alex and Casey sat down in the back of the ambulance as the door was closed and they started the ride to the hospital.

In the ambulance, they decided to remove their NASA flight suits. Alex helped Riley with hers as it wasn't easy to get out of it while lying on a bed.

'Wow, that feels better,' said Casey. 'Those things can feel claustrophobic after a while.'

'How are you feeling now?' Alex asked Riley.

'Alright, thanks,' she replied. 'I'm regaining my strength but I have got some pain in my back.'

Once they arrived at the Walter Reed Hospital, they were taken straight through to see a doctor. After about an hour, during which time they were all examined and checked for external and internal injuries, they were told they could go.

'You're all okay as far as we can tell,' said the doctor. 'You could all do with a couple of days rest though,' he added.

'That we can agree on, Doctor,' said Alex.

'Riley,' said the doctor, 'you may have pulled some muscles in your back so some physio may help.'

'Okay, Doctor,' said Riley.

They contacted Director Andrews to find out where they should go next.

'Home,' he said. 'I'll send a car for you at 10.00 a.m. tomorrow, but until then get some rest.'

'Thank you, sir,' said Riley on the phone. 'We're going to Arlington,' she told the others.

'Great,' said Casey, 'a night in my own bed!'

They went outside the hospital and flagged down a taxi. Climbing in, the three of them asked to go to Lee Heights in Arlington, Virginia. The taxi set off winding its way through the crowded city streets.

'There's so many people here,' said Riley.

'Well it is the fourth of July!' replied Alex.

'Happy Independence Day,' said Casey.

'Yeah, happy fourth everyone,' said Riley.

It wasn't long before they were arriving back home at their little house in Arlington. Elsie was there to meet them.

'Welcome home, guys,' she said as they walked in. They all looked exhausted and after what they'd been through, that wasn't surprising. Riley had probably only managed about four hours sleep during the transatlantic flights.

'Why don't you all have showers and put your PJs on? 'I'll prepare you a little fourth of July dinner,' she said, smiling.

'Okay, thanks, Elsie,' said Riley.

They left the NASA flight packs in the hallway and made their way upstairs. Their rooms were just as they'd left them, except Elsie had put fresh sheets on all the beds and hung clean towels ready for their return.

'Who's first?' said Alex.

'Not you,' replied Casey, 'you take too long!'

Riley laughed. 'I'll go first if that's okay,' she said.

'Yeah, that's fine, you've been catching missiles and crashing helicopters. We've just flown around a bit!' said Casey, smiling.

'Flown around dodging bullets!' replied Riley.

'True,' said Casey, 'but you've still earned first spot.'

'Okay,' replied Riley.

She went into her room and took off her clothes. Wrapping her towel round her, she came back to the landing to make her way to the bathroom to find the others still stood there talking.

'Oh, excuse me,' she said, sounding a little embarrassed, as she slipped past them and into the bathroom. Alex's glance followed her as she walked to the bathroom, something Casey was quick to spot.

'You do like her, don't you?' Casey said to him.

'Yeah I do,' he replied.

'I don't blame you,' she added, smiling. 'You should tell her,' said Casey.

'You wouldn't mind?' asked Alex. 'I know you have feelings for her too.'

'No, I don't mind and yeah, I do have feelings for her, but I love you both and want you to be happy,' said Casey.

'Thanks, Casey, I'll talk to her later,' said Alex.

Riley was now in the shower and it had never felt so good to be clean. As she stood there with shampoo and water trickling over her skin, she thought about everything that had happened since her last shower. There had been an incredible amount, starting with a day in the London school and an MI5 briefing. Then an undercover operation in the London terror cell that led to an emergency meeting at Thames House. This led to two helicopter flights either side of a jet plane that stopped on an aircraft carrier. Then if all that wasn't enough, she stopped a missile from hitting the White House and brought down a helicopter filled with terrorists before controlling an explosion on the White House lawn! She put some shower gel in the palm of her hand and gently rubbed it onto her skin. Wishing she could stand there forever, she suddenly remembered the others were in a queue waiting to use the bathroom. She quickly rinsed off the remaining suds before turning the water off and stepping out of the cubicle. Grabbing her towel, she rubbed the worst of the water from her hair before wrapping herself back up in the towel. She made her way onto a now empty landing with her wet hair hanging loose down her back.

'Bathroom's free,' she shouted as she disappeared into her room to get her pyjamas on.

Alex went next and was equally pleased to finally feel clean again. Casey went last as she knew the pressure to be quick would no longer apply. Riley was sitting in her pyjama vest and shorts on the sofa when Alex walked into the lounge.

'How come you're in here?' he asked.

'Oh, Elsie wants the kitchen to herself to prepare a surprise,' said Riley.

'Can I sit down?' asked Alex coming to the sofa, rather than his usual armchair.

'Yeah, sure,' said Riley sliding up to make space for him.

'Thanks,' he said, as he sat down. 'I wanted to talk to you.'

'Oh,' said Riley, 'what about?' She was pretty sure she knew, well she hoped she knew.

'I wanted to talk about us, as in you and me,' he said. Riley's heart jumped inside her chest. Her brain stepped in though and said to her to play it cool!

'What about us?' she asked.

Alex moved back on the sofa to its arm and turned sideways to face her. She did the same at the other end of the two-seater. They were now sat cross-legged and facing one another.

'Well,' said Alex taking a deep breath, 'we've had a couple of little moments in the last twenty-four hours.'

'Yeah, we have,' she said, smiling.

'Firstly, holding hands on the aircraft carrier flight deck and then that kiss on the White House lawn,' he said.

She smiled at him and said, 'So what are you saying?'

He paused for a moment as if trying to find some inner courage. 'I'm saying, would you like to be my girlfriend?'

he replied.

He looked at her with an anxious expression. She could see this in his eyes and reached forward to hold his hands.

'Of course I would!' she replied with a smile.

Alex breathed a sigh of relief. Riley pulled him closer and put her arms around his neck. She then kissed him. He placed his hands on her hips and they stayed there for a moment. Then, Casey walked in and sat in the armchair.

She sat there for a moment before she said, 'Oh don't mind me!'

Riley and Alex flew apart, both turning bright red. They turned on the sofa dropping their feet to the floor to face Casey.

'I see you've had your little chat then, Alex!' said Casey.

'Yeah,' said Alex, still glowing crimson.

'You knew about this?' said Riley.

'Of course, who do you think encouraged him to ask you out!' replied Casey.

'Aw, thanks, Casey,' said Riley, getting up and going over to give her friend a hug.

'Right you three, dinner time,' said Elsie, appearing in the doorway.

The three of them got up and followed her to the kitchen. Alex took Riley by the hand on the way there. As they walked in, a wonderful sight greeted their eyes.

'Wow,' said Riley.

Elsie had made their favourite meal of burgers and fries. But, in the spirit of the day, each burger had a lit sparkler sticking from it, showering their plates with twinkling light.

'Aw, thanks, Elsie,' said Casey. 'These look great.'

'My pleasure,' replied Elsie.

They all sat down and tucked into the food. They were all very hungry after such a busy couple of days.

After dinner, Elsie cleared away the plates and then said her goodbyes.

'I'll see you in the morning,' she said. 'Make sure you all get a good night's sleep.'

'We will, thanks, Elsie,' said Casey.

Once she'd left, they all made their way upstairs.

'I'll see you guys in the morning,' said Casey yawning. She hugged them both then went to the bathroom to brush her teeth. Riley took hold of Alex's hand,

'You okay to come in for a few minutes?' she said.

'Yeah, sure,' he replied as they walked towards her bedroom. She led him to the bed and they both climbed on and sat leaning against the headboard.

'Thanks for asking me out,' she said.

'My pleasure,' replied Alex, smiling.

'I was hoping you would,' she said.

'I kinda picked that up,' he replied.

She put her arm across his chest and kissed him on the cheek. He turned his head to face her and kissed her on the lips.

'There was something else I wanted to say,' she said.

'Oh, what's that?' asked Alex.

'I wanted to thank you for saving my life. I could have fallen into that helicopter wreckage if you'd not caught me,' said Riley.

'I was just glad I got to you in time,' he said.

'Me too,' she said, kissing him again.

'We should call it a night,' said Alex. 'We both need the sleep and no doubt Director Andrews will keep us busy tomorrow.'

'Yeah, you're right,' replied Riley.

She stood up and walked round the bed. He did the same and they met at her bedroom door. Hugging her, he said goodnight before heading to his own room. Riley brushed her teeth in the bathroom before getting into bed. *Wow,* she thought, *Casey was right. It did feel good to be back in her own bed!* Riley smiled to herself as she closed her eyes. What an amazing fourth of July it had been.

Chapter 25

Langley

Alex was the first to wake on Saturday morning. The sun was shining and all seemed well with the world as he got himself up out of bed. *I am looking forward to a Saturday when I can just stay in bed,* he thought as he remembered they were being collected for a debriefing with the CIA at Langley in a few hours. As he finished in the bathroom, he knocked on the girls' doors to check they were awake.

Everyone appeared around the same time downstairs in the kitchen where Elsie was already busy making breakfast.

'Here,' said Riley, 'let me sort the coffee, Elsie.'

'Thank you dear, that would be helpful,' replied Elsie. Riley filled the kettle to heat the water. The others set the table. At last everything was ready and they all sat down.

'So, have you got another busy day ahead of you?' asked Elsie.

'We have,' said Casey.

'Although I'm not too sure exactly what we will be doing,' added Riley.

'I expect it will be a lot of interviews and report writing,' said Alex.

'So, like being at school then!' said Casey in a slightly depressed tone.

After breakfast they helped clear away before going back upstairs to brush their teeth. Alex took hold of Riley's hand as Casey went into the bathroom.

'Hey you,' he said, as she turned towards him, 'how are you feeling this morning?'

'Good, thanks,' she replied before kissing him. Casey reappeared at that moment as she'd left something in her room.

'Gee, you two!' she said. They stopped kissing and started laughing.

'Sorry, Casey,' said Riley, 'we should be more considerate.'

'You should,' she said, 'but don't let me stop you. I'm glad my two best friends are so happy.'

Riley and Alex let go of each other on one side and pulled Casey in for a three-way hug.

'Don't get all mushy on me now!' said Casey.

'We won't,' said Alex, 'but it is nice to have best friends.'

'What about your friend Will from college?' asked Riley.

'Yeah, he's a best buddy, but I can't share everything with him. I can with you two,' said Alex.

'Yeah, I guess that does make our friendship unique,' said Casey.

'Now who's getting mushy?' said Riley.

'Yeah right,' said Casey breaking free of the hug. 'Come on, we need to be ready for our ride,' she added.

Shortly after 10.00 a.m. Agent Jacobs arrived.

'Morning all,' said Agent Jacobs as they got into the car. He turned to Casey in the back and asked, 'Is Riley here?'

'She's next to you!' said Casey. She was confused by his comment as Riley wasn't invisible. Agent Jacobs looked at Riley and then at the seat she was in.

'Are you sure she's here?' he said laughing.

'Very funny,' said Riley, whacking him on the shoulder. The others were already laughing in the back, as was Agent Jacobs.

'We've missed our morning runs with you,' said Casey.

'Likewise,' said Agent Jacobs, 'I'm glad you're all back here safe.'

'So are we,' said Alex.

Agent Jacobs drove them through the streets of Arlington and out of town to Langley and the headquarters of the Central Intelligence Agency. On arrival they were met by James, who'd travelled to London with them.

'Morning, guys. I hope you're feeling rested.'

'We are, thanks,' said Alex.

'Well done for saving the White House, oh and the thousands of people at the Capitol yesterday,' said James.

'Thanks,' replied Riley. She'd not stopped to think just how many people were safe because of her bravery yesterday. It was kind of mind-blowing.

James took them through to a large conference room with a huge oval shaped table.

'Take a seat, guys, I'll let Director Andrews know you're here,' said James.

As he left the room someone wheeled in a trolley with coffee and cake on.

Riley looked at the others and quietly mouthed, 'What's that all about?' It was unusual for an intelligence briefing to have coffee and cake.

The answer to Riley's question came very quickly as Director Andrews entered the room with the President of the United States, his Chief of Staff, the National Security Advisor, and the Directors of the FBI and CIA. Riley and the others stood up as soon as they saw the President.

'Sit down, sit down,' he said as he took the chair at the head of the table. Riley, Casey and Alex, were sitting in a row on his right and the others were opposite them.

The lady who'd brought in the trolley went about serving coffee and cake to those who wanted it, while Director Andrews opened the meeting.

'Sir, thank you for taking time out from your busy schedule to join us this morning,' he said.

'Not at all, Jack, I had to after what these three did yesterday to protect the White House, and thousands of American citizens, not to mention the work they did in London that prevented the destruction of the British parliament,' replied the President.

'Well, thank you, sir,' repeated Director Andrews.

'I'm aware that you have a number of major security issues to discuss,' said the President, 'including the breach in Capitol security. But before you begin, I wanted to thank you all for your efforts and discuss how we might honour Riley for her exceptional bravery.'

Riley went bright red. Alex took hold of her hand under the table sensing how embarrassed she was feeling.

'Sir,' said Director Andrews, 'if we go public with this, we will have to deal with a lot of questions, most notably from her family. Can you give us some time to discuss this as agency heads? We can then assess the impact it would have on future operations.'

'Absolutely, Jack,' said the President, 'but either way I'd like you, Riley, Casey and Alex at the White House tonight for dinner.'

'Yes, sir,' replied Jack, looking at Riley and co., who were all nodding.

They knew dinner with the President was a real honour in itself and if that were all the thanks they got, it would be more than enough.

'Great, well that's all from me for now,' said the President. 'I'll leave you all to get on with the real work.'

With that, he and his Chief of Staff got up to leave. Everyone around the table stood as he walked out before retaking their seats.

'Riley, we will discuss the President's proposal a little later,' said Director Andrews. 'Before that, we need to go through Operation Legion to make sure we have all the facts right.'

'Of course, sir,' replied Riley.

'Right,' said Jack, 'first of all, thanks, Rohan, for the use of your building this morning.'

'No problem,' replied the CIA Director.

'Let's review the operation, shall we?' added Jack.

Rohan started off, 'Well, from our perspective it was a great success. Riley and co worked well with James which meant the international aspect of the operation ran smoothly. The training they'd received beforehand certainly paid off as the intel gathered on both sides of the Atlantic proved invaluable.'

'Thanks, Rohan,' replied Director Andrews.

'From a national security perspective,' said the FBI Director, 'the intel again was brilliant. We will however, be continuing our investigation into the leak at the Capitol. I wasn't pleased to be kept out of the loop regarding the final operation in DC,' he added, 'but under the circumstances I appreciate why that decision was made.'

'Thanks, Luca,' replied Jack.

'Riley, have you got anything you want to add?' asked Director Andrews.

'Only to thank everyone for the support we've had doing this,' she said. 'Oh, and whoever decided to retrofit my flight suit with thrusters deserves a medal. Without that I couldn't have lifted Wendy out of the crowd and flown away at the same time.'

'We will have to thank Commander Adams at NASA for that one,' said Jack. 'She thought you might need your energy pulse, or just your hands, for something other than flight.'

'Well she was right,' said Riley, 'and it helped save a lot of lives.'

'I have a question,' said Alex.

'Go on,' said Jack.

'It's actually a CIA question for Director Montgomery.'

Rohan sat up in his chair. 'Fire away,' he said.

'I presume we shared all our intel with MI5. So, who provided the inside help? The only way those bomb parts could be in the parliament building before the terrorists is if they had inside help,' said Alex.

'Good question and yes, we did,' said Rohan.

'It's clear there's been some inside help for both terror cells here, and in London,' said Director Andrews, 'but that's now a task for the FBI and MI5 to handle on a domestic level.'

'Thank you, sir,' said Alex.

'Gentlemen, if that is all, I need to have a discussion with Riley, Casey and Alex about their positions in the Secret Service,' said Director Andrews.

'Of course,' said Rohan, Luca and Steve, getting up to leave the room.

Jack got up and poured a coffee.

'Anyone want one?' he asked. All three of them replied, 'yes, please!'

The Director poured four cups and brought them to the table. Taking his seat once again, he looked across the table at the three of them. They looked back with anxious expressions.

'Why are you all looking so worried?' asked Director Andrews.

'I guess we are worried this is the end of our service!' said Riley. Alex squeezed her hand under the table.

'Well stop worrying,' said the Director, 'I'd be a fool to let three of our best agents go!'

They all breathed a sigh of relief.

'We do need to decide how public we make your appointments. Also, what we tell your families,' he added.

'Do you mean my invisibly and so on?' asked Riley.

'No,' said the Director, 'that needs to remain classified. But it would be easier to take you away from home for long periods if your parents were in the loop.'

'Hmm,' said Casey, 'there's two sides to that argument. Our parents knowing is good, especially if something happened to us. But, them knowing may make things worse as they maybe too scared to let us do what we do.'

'You've hit the nail on the head,' said Jack, 'and that's why I want the three of you to discuss this and let me know on Monday. You know your families better than we do,' he said.

'Okay, sir,' said Riley, 'we will talk about it and let you know.'

After they'd spent an hour or so typing up mission reports for the Director, they were taken back to Arlington so they could have a few hours to get ready for dinner in the White House.

'How am I gonna get ready in just a few hours?' said Casey, laughing in the car.

'Brush your hair and put a Nirvana t-shirt on and you'll be sorted,' replied Alex, for which he got a clip round the ear!

Chapter 26

Decisions

Back at the house at Lee Heights, they made some drinks and sat together in the lounge. Casey took the armchair this time so Riley could sit with Alex.

'We need to think hard about this,' said Riley.

'Yeah, telling our parents is a big deal,' said Casey.

'Why is it they want to tell them anyway?' asked Riley.

'They think it'll make life easier in the future if our parents know what we do for the Secret Service,' replied Alex.

'You see, I'm not sure it will,' said Riley, 'as Casey said at the CIA meeting, if our parents know they may be too scared to let us be agents.'

Riley stood up and paced up and down.

'What are you thinking?' asked Alex.

'I'm thinking it would be nice not to have to keep this a secret from my mom,' she replied.

'But isn't that why we are in the Secret Service?' said Casey. 'Because some things are meant to be kept secret to protect the public.'

'I guess so,' said Riley. 'What do you think, Alex?'

'If we did tell our parents, what would we say? I mean would your mom believe you if you said you'd caught a missile in mid-flight and downed a helicopter full of terrorists? Oh, and twelve hours before that you were in a jet landing on a British aircraft carrier in the Atlantic!' he said.

'When you put it like that,' said Riley, 'yeah my mom wouldn't believe a word of it.'

'So why tell them then?' said Alex.

'He's got a point, you know,' said Casey.

'Yeah, I know,' said Riley.

'The other issue is the President wants the publicity from

161

this,' said Casey. 'He wants some national heroes to parade before the cameras.'

'I understand that,' said Alex, 'but if we become that, we lose our effectiveness as Secret Service special agents. I'm not sure I'm prepared to do that.'

The girls agreed with him. Neither of them wanted to be in the limelight and risk being useless for future operations.

'So, are we decided then?' said Alex,

'I think so,' said Riley, clearly still running it all through her mind.

Casey seemed more certain. 'Yes, we're clear,' she said.

'We will tell the President and Director Andrews tonight that we don't want our parents to know more than they do and we want our role as Secret Service agents to remain secret,' said Alex.

'What if the President asks about publicly thanking us?' said Riley.

'Then we tell him to publicly thank Director Andrews and his team,' said Casey.

'We can also say that having dinner with them both is more than thanks enough,' added Riley.

'Cheesy,' said Casey, laughing.

'Oh, shut up!' said Riley sitting back down next to Alex.

'Talking of dinner, hadn't we better start getting ready?' said Alex.

'Yeah, we had,' said Riley.

'I'm first in the bathroom!' said Casey, jumping up from the armchair.

'Fine by us,' said Riley.

'Of course it is,' said Casey, 'it gives you two some cuddle time!'

'Now who's being cheesy,' replied Alex as Casey left the room laughing.

Riley looked at Alex. 'She's not wrong though,' said Riley as she snuggled in next to him on the sofa.

When Casey had finished in the bathroom, she gave Riley a shout. Riley did the same for Alex. They always made him go last if they could as he had got a reputation for taking ages! Casey knocked on Riley's door.

'Come in,' she said. Riley was sitting in her dressing gown at her dressing table putting on a little makeup in the mirror.

'Oh, hi Casey,' she said, 'what can I do for you?'

'Actually, I was coming to ask you the same,' said Casey. 'Would you like me to do your hair for you?'

Riley turned around on her chair to face her friend. 'Yes, please,' she replied.

Casey walked over. 'What can I do for you?' she asked.

Riley thought for a moment. 'Could you do a single French plait?' she replied.

'Of course,' said Casey, picking up the hairbrush. Riley liked it when Casey did this. It was like having a big sister. Riley would never let Beth near her hair for fear it might all be cut off, or worse!

At last they were all ready. Riley was in a dark blue off-the-shoulder dress that came down to just above the knee. It had short sleeves and she was wearing a thin gold chain round her neck.

'Wow,' said Alex when she appeared in the hall, 'you look stunning!'

'Thanks,' said Riley, blushing.

Alex had put on a dark red shirt and some black jeans. Casey was surprised how smart in he looked in them.

'Jeans? Really?' she said.

'Smart jeans,' replied Alex.

'I guess,' said Casey.

Casey had also put on a dress. Hers was a soft green colour with a subtle flowery pattern on. It had shoulder straps and was a little longer than Riley's, stopping just below the knee. Not her normal style, but it seemed to suit her.

'Love the dress,' said Riley.

'Yeah, Mom got it for me last year,' said Casey. 'Been putting off wearing it,' she added, laughing.

Shortly after they'd finished admiring each other's outfits, the doorbell rang. An agent they didn't recognise said she was there to take them to the White House.

'Where's Agent Jacobs?' asked Casey on the way across the Potomac.

'Oh, off duty,' replied the female agent. 'He's back in tomorrow.'

It didn't take long to arrive at the White House. Director Andrews met them and escorted them to the residence and the President's private dining room.

'Good evening, everyone,' said the President, as they walked in. 'Please do sit down.'

They all sat round the circular table set for five people. Riley sat with Alex on her left and the President on her right. Casey was on the President's right and Director Andrews sat between Casey and Alex. A member of the kitchen staff came through to serve them their first course, which was a light seafood salad. Casey, who wasn't a fan of mussels, managed to hide the fact well and downed them all. Fortunately, only Riley spotted her twisted face every time she swallowed the slippery suckers!

'So, tell me, have you guys chatted about sharing what you do for us with your parents?' asked the President. Director Andrews, stepped in before they could answer.

'Sir, I did give them until Monday to consider this.'

'It's okay, sir,' said Riley to Jack, 'we've come to a decision already.'

'Oh,' said Jack.

'What have you decided?' asked the President. Riley hesitated, so Alex spoke up.

'We want to remain secret, sir,' he said. 'No publicity, no parent involvement.'

'Really?' said the President.

'Yes, sir,' said Riley, finding her voice. 'We want to remain as effective as we have been in this operation and we feel keeping what we do a secret is the best way for us to serve you and the nation.'

'Well, you can't argue with that, sir!' said Jack.

'No, Jack, I can't,' said the President. 'It does leave me with the issues of publicly thanking you for what you've done,' he added.

'Not really, sir,' said Casey, 'just thank Director Andrews and his team, and the joint partnership with the FBI, CIA and MI5.'

'As for us, sir,' said Riley, 'dinner here is more than we could have imagined and that's thanks enough.'

The President paused a moment as if considering everything they'd said.

'Very well. You are all correct, it does leave you in a better position to continue working for the Secret Service. Jack, if you're happy with this, I'm happy to keep their cover intact, including with their parents.'

'More than happy, sir,' said Jack. 'They're one of my best teams. I'd hate to jeopardise that for the sake of publicity.'

'Okay,' said the President, 'in that case, this is a thank you dinner for saving us once again!'

'Thank you, sir,' said Riley.

The kitchen staff cleared the starter and brought through the main course of Texas steaks. Everyone tucked into the food.

'Oh, by the way, guys, you have a day off tomorrow,' said Jack, 'then the rest of the week you'll be visiting various middle schools as White House Ambassadors. We need to give you something to talk to your families about when you go home!' he said, smiling.

'Thanks, sir,' said Alex.

At the end of dinner, the President thanked them once again for their courage and bravery and said he looked forward to seeing them again in the future. They then left the White House and headed back to the house in Lee Heights. Collapsing onto the sofa, Riley and Casey looked at Alex.

'Please can you make some coffees?' they asked. Their puppy dog eyes worked a treated and he gave in without a fight.

'Okay yeah,' he said, going off to the kitchen.

This gave the girls some time alone.

'So?' said Casey.

'So, what?' asked Riley.

'So, is Alex a good kisser?' asked Casey. Riley frowned at her. 'Well, is he?' asked Casey again.

Riley sighed, realising she wasn't gonna give up asking. 'Yeah, he's good,' she replied.

'Better than me?' asked Casey.

'Now that's not fair,' said Riley. 'I'm not gonna have this conversation and I'd never compare you both anyway!'

'Okay fair enough, sorry,' said Casey.

'Sorry for what?' asked Alex, walking in with a tray of coffees.

'Oh, nothing,' said Casey trying to sound sweet and innocent.

'Yeah, right,' said Alex. He knew when to drop something as he knew the girls wouldn't share their conversation with him.

Sitting down, he decided to start a new conversation. 'We do need to make one more decision regarding parents,' he said.

'Oh, what's that?' said Riley.

'Telling them you have a boyfriend!' he replied, smiling.

'Oh my,' she said. 'I wonder how my mom will react to that!'

'Probably better than hearing you'd caught a missile in mid-flight,' said Alex.

'Oh, I don't know, I think the missile story would have been easier!' she replied, laughing.

Casey started laughing too but Alex didn't.

'Oh, come on Alex, that was funny,' said Casey. He relaxed a bit and smiled.

'But seriously,' he said, 'are you gonna tell your mom?'

'Yeah of course,' said Riley. 'I just need to figure out what to say as this is a first for me. Casey and I didn't tell anyone except you,' she added.

'Fair enough,' said Alex. 'I'm in the same situation as you're my first girlfriend. I have a feeling my dad will be pleased though, as he thinks the world of you and Casey.'

'I didn't know that,' said Riley, smiling.

'Yeah, he says I'm more like the boy I used to be before Mom died, when I'm with you two. I'm guessing that's a good thing,' replied Alex. Riley got up and gave him a hug.

'Thanks for telling us that,' she said.

Not one for too much emotion, Casey was keen to move the conversation on.

'Any thoughts on what we do tomorrow?' she said.

'A touristy day in Washington would be good,' replied Riley.

'Yeah,' said Alex, 'perhaps visit some places we've not seen yet.'

'Sounds good,' said Casey, 'any thoughts on where?'

'Perhaps we could check out some of the museums we've not seen yet,' said Alex.

'I'd quite like to visit Arlington House,' said Riley, 'after all we've been living in Lee Heights for weeks and it's nearby.'

'Okay,' said Alex, 'how about you, Casey?'

'I don't mind, just be good to have a day with you two where we aren't having to save the world!' she said smiling. The others agreed.

Chapter 27

Tourists for A Day

'Well, it's getting late,' said Casey, 'so I'm turning in. I'll see you both in the morning.'

The others said goodnight and Casey left them on the sofa to go upstairs.

'We'd better not stay up too late,' said Riley.

'Okay,' said Alex, 'just for a little bit then.'

Riley took off her shoes and put her bare feet and legs across Alex's lap on the sofa.

'I'm a foot rest now, am I?' he said, smiling.

'A very handsome one, yes,' replied Riley. Alex put his hands on her feet and ran them along her legs to her knees and back again.

'That feels nice,' she said. So he kept doing it while they sat talking.

'When do you think they'll send us home?' she asked.

'I don't know,' said Alex, 'but I'm guessing fairly soon.'

'Why do you say that?' she asked.

'Because, we've done most of the training,' he said. 'Also, we've completed the mission they needed us on. I'm guessing once we have evidence for our cover story we will be going back to our separate homes.'

'Oh, don't say that!' she said. 'I hate the idea of being separated from you and Casey after all we've done together. I've kinda gotten used to living together. I love seeing you at the very start and end of each day.'

'I feel the same,' replied Alex, 'but the reality is we have families that miss us and we need to get back to them. Besides, we spend most of our free time together and that won't change.'

'True,' said Riley, 'but moments like this will be harder to come by.'

'So let's make the most of them,' replied Alex.

Riley put her feet down and turned herself around so she could kiss him. They cuddled on the sofa for a while, before Alex finally said, 'We need to get some sleep.'

'Okay,' she said, sounding reluctant to move.

They got up and made their way upstairs, having one last kiss on the landing before saying goodnight and heading to their rooms.

Riley unzipped her dress and made sure it went back on a hanger before she put on her pyjamas and got into bed. Having a boyfriend was great and she was pleased it was Alex. She lay in bed thinking about him and Casey and felt thankful for everything that had happened to bring the three of them together.

In the morning the three of them got up and dressed at a reasonable time. Well, around 10.00 a.m. which for a teenager at the weekend is exceptional rather than reasonable!

'I'm glad no-one is sleeping in today or we'd never get our touristy things done,' said Casey.

'Good morning to you too!' said Riley.

After breakfast they ordered a taxi to take them to Arlington House and the National Cemetery. They decided to start there and then head over the Potomac to Washington. The taxi wound its way through the cemetery to the house at the top of the hill. Once the home of Robert E Lee, the house was now a museum and visitor centre to the National Cemetery. They paid the driver and got out of the taxi.

'Shall we take a look round the museum first?' suggested Alex.

'Sounds good to me,' said Casey as the three of them walked inside.

They spent a good hour looking round, especially at the paintings of Lee and George Washington.

'Wow,' said Casey, 'I had no idea one little house could have so much history in it.'

'Little?' replied Riley.

'Well, you know what I mean.'

After their look around the museum they visited some of the heroes in the cemetery. They all wanted to pay their respects to the Challenger Space Shuttle crew, having had part of their training at NASA.

Early in the afternoon they took another taxi across the Potomac River and into Washington itself. There they stopped at the Lincoln Memorial before starting their long walk down the Mall to the Smithsonian Museums.

'You know what,' said Riley, 'flying along here in an anti-gravity suit is so much easier than walking!'

The others laughed at her, but completely agreed it was a long walk!

It took some persuasion but the girls managed to convince Alex not to make a beeline straight for the Air and Space Museum to start with.

'Okay, which one then?' he asked.

'Let's go to the National Art Gallery,' said Riley.

'Then the Natural History Museum,' said Casey.

'Okay, I'm happy with that,' said Alex, 'at least I'll get to see dinosaurs!'

'Such a geek,' said Casey, shaking her head at him.

Riley just laughed and put her arm round Alex to console him. Once inside the National Gallery they decided to have a drink in its cafe before looking around.

'It is after 1.00 p.m. and we've not stopped yet,' explained Casey, as she pitched for a drinks break.

'Yeah that's fine,' said Riley, 'I could do with a break before we walk any further.'

The girls had some strawberry milkshakes, like they used to in the cafe near the library back home. Alex had his usual coffee.

'So,' said Alex, 'you're the artist amongst us, where do we start, Riley?'

She'd picked up a guide leaflet up on their way in so opened it to get some inspiration before answering Alex.

'Let's take a look at the Leonardo da Vinci paintings,' said Riley.

They spent another hour wandering the halls of the

museum. Riley was in her element. She loved seeing art and wondering what the artist had been thinking when they created the piece. She would imagine herself working in the studio, alongside the great masters. She aspired to be like them but wondered if she'd ever be as good.

'What are you thinking?' asked Alex as he watched Riley staring at a painting of George Washington.

'Oh, I'm just wondering if I'll ever be able to paint like this,' she replied.

'One thing I know about you,' said Alex, 'is that if you put your mind to it, you can achieve anything.'

She put her arm round his shoulder and kissed him on the cheek.

'Thank you,' she said.

'Hey, none of that in here, you two,' said Casey, smiling at them.

'You ready for some dinosaurs?' asked Riley to Alex.

'Always,' he replied.

'Come on then my lovely geek, let's go!' she said taking his hand.

He thought about replying, but to be honest was content with her description of him as it was fairly accurate. Casey followed them as the three headed out of the Art Gallery and turned right back towards the Washington Monument.

'Is there any reason we didn't do these museums the other way around?' asked Casey. 'It would have saved walking back on ourselves.'

'Yeah, true,' said Riley, 'but that's being organised and we're being tourists!'

'There is such a thing as an organised tourist, you know!' replied Casey.

'That's not us though, is it?' said Alex, laughing.

'Clearly,' said Casey.

It didn't take them too long to reach the main entrance of the Natural History Museum. Alex seemed to find a new lease of life as they arrived and the girls had to tell him to slow down so they could keep up. Once inside, Alex was like a kid in a candy store. Whichever way he turned, his eyes were popping out of his head.

'Calm down,' said Riley, 'we've got several hours before it closes. That's plenty of time to have a good look round.'

They spent the rest of their day pottering around the Natural History Museum. When it closed at 6.00 p.m., they decided to find somewhere in Arlington to eat out for the evening. They'd let Elsie know they'd be having tea out so she wouldn't be making a meal unnecessarily.

'So where shall we eat?' said Riley as they walked along.

'How about here,' said Casey pointing at a restaurant called The Liberty Tavern. They stopped and looked at the menu.

'This looks good. Shall we try it?' said Riley.

'Yeah, why not,' said Alex. So the three of them went in and found a table.

Choosing something other than burgers, they all picked a main course and a desert. It was great to end their day out like this.

'We really have been tourists today, haven't we?' said Riley.

'Yeah, it's been good fun,' said Casey.

'Tiring, but good fun,' added Alex.

At the end of the meal, Alex offered to pay for everyone.

'Thanks, that's really sweet of you,' said Riley.

They left the restaurant and made their way back to the house in Lee Heights. It was about 9.30 p.m. when they got in. Casey made some coffees and they spent the rest of the evening chilling out and chatting together in the lounge. Riley put the television on and the news came up on screen.

'Repeating our story from earlier,' said the reporter, 'the President addressed the nation this morning following a foiled terror attack on Washington DC and London.'

The screen then changed to the President's address.

'My fellow Americans, I am pleased to be able to tell you that, thanks to Director Andrews and his unique team of special agents, plus a joint task force involving the FBI, CIA, MI5 and the Secret Service, we are no longer at risk from a terrorist group known as the First World Order.'

The report went on to detail how a missile had been neutralised and a helicopter brought down. It also told the public that bombers in London and Washington had been prevented from completing their mission. Riley, Casey and Alex, watched with interest as the report shared the amazing events without giving away any of what they'd done or who they were. At the end of the broadcast Riley switched off the television.

'Well, they've honoured their word and kept us classified,' she said.

'Here's to many more successful missions,' said Casey, raising her coffee cup.

At around 11.00 p.m. Casey said she was going to bed and told the others to not stay up too late.

'Yes, Mom!' replied Alex. Casey gave him an unimpressed look as she left the room.

'Do you want to stay here?' said Riley after Casey had gone up to bed.

'Where else would we go?' replied Alex.

'We could go to my room,' said Riley.

'Okay,' said Alex.

The two of them got up and held hands as they climbed the stairs. On the landing Riley suggested they put their pyjamas on.

'Okay,' said Alex, 'but I wanna make it clear we aren't doing anything. We are both under eighteen and we've only just started dating.'

'Aw, thanks,' replied Riley, 'you're so sweet. That's fine with me. I don't want to rush things either. It'll just be nice to have a cuddle.' Alex relaxed a bit.

'Okay, I'll see you in a moment,' he said.

Riley went into her room and took her clothes off. She found her pyjama shorts and vest and put them on then sat on her bed and waited. It wasn't long before Alex appeared. He left the door open as he came in which Riley was pleased about. She took it to mean he planned to keep his word about not doing anything. He climbed on to the bed and she slid down so they could lie next to one another.

They lay facing each other.

'You are beautiful,' said Alex. Riley smiled.

'So are you,' she replied, not quite sure what else to say. He laughed a little.

'Not something anyone has called me before,' he said.

'Likewise,' she replied.

He leant in to kiss her. She moved closer to him so their bodies were touching. They put an arm round each other. He stopped kissing her lips and started to kiss her neck.

'That's nice,' she said. She lifted her leg onto his, which pushed him onto his back. Then moving over, she lay on top of him and kissed him.

Not wanting to rush things, Alex just hugged her like this for a while before stopping. They went back to lying facing each other and talked for a while.

'Thanks for respecting me and not rushing things,' she said.

'Likewise,' said Alex, 'I care about you more than I can put into words. I don't want to spoil that.'

'I feel the same,' she said.

They spent a little longer just being together before Alex said goodnight and went to his own room. Getting into bed that night, Riley felt so happy. Her life was finally becoming something she'd only ever dreamed about.

Chapter 28

Youth Ambassadors

Monday morning came all too quickly. Riley, Casey and Alex were eating breakfast when the doorbell rang. Elsie opened the door to let Agent Jacobs in.

'Morning, guys,' he said.

'Oh hi, long time no see,' said Casey.

'Yeah, it's been a while,' replied Agent Jacobs, 'you lot ready?'

'Yes,' said Riley.

They followed Agent Jacobs to the car. Once inside Alex asked, 'Which school are we in today?'

'The Jefferson Middle School,' replied Agent Jacobs. 'I believe you'll be working with grade eight kids on staying safe on the streets.'

'I wonder if we can teach them some of Koba's martial arts moves!' said Casey jokingly. The others just looked at her disapprovingly.

The middle school was only across the river from Arlington so it didn't take them long to reach it.

'Oh, I nearly forgot,' said Agent Jacobs, handing them some lanyards with I.D. badges on.

'These are your White House Youth Ambassador I.D.s,' he said.

'Thanks,' said Riley as she took her badge and looked at it. They'd used the photographs from their Secret Service badges to create some alternative identification for them.

Riley, Casey and Alex got out of the car and made their way into the school. They were met inside by one of the teachers.

'Hi guys, are you the team from the White House?' she asked.

'Yes,' replied Riley, 'I'm Riley, this is Casey and Alex.'

'Oh yes,' said the teacher, 'everyone knows your names

at this school, especially after you saved the President's life.'

The three of them just smiled, not sure how to reply to this.

'Right,' said the teacher, 'the first class will be ready for you by now. We will start with introductions and a quick question and answer session. Then it's over to you guys to talk about staying safe on the streets.'

'Okay,' said Alex.

Although the three of them felt a little bit like they'd been dropped in at the deep end, they knew that they could handle this. In Riley's head there was a small battle raging between two different thoughts. The first was a doubting thought that claimed she wasn't up to standing in front of a class and saying anything, even if it was a class of eighth graders. The other thought was a confident one that claimed she could handle anything. She was the girl who'd saved the President, caught a missile in mid-air and brought down a helicopter. What could eighth graders do to her?

They followed the teacher into the classroom, which was packed with about twenty-five twelve and thirteen-year-olds.

'Morning, class,' said the teacher.

'Morning, Miss,' came the response from about five of them.

'We have some visitors with us from the White House today,' said the teacher. She then proceeded to introduce Riley and her friends.

'Now,' said the teacher, 'I'm going to give you the opportunity to asked sensible questions. Does anyone have a question for our visitors?'

There was silence for a moment then one of the girls put their hand up.

'Yes, Ava,' said the teacher.

'Did you guys really stop a bullet from killing the President?'

Alex decided to speak first and answer. 'Yes, we did,' he said, 'although it was actually Riley who jumped in front of the gunman.'

'So did the bullet hit you?' asked Ava.

'Yes, it did,' said Riley.

'Did it hurt?' asked Ava.

'Yes, it did,' replied Riley.

'Okay Ava, that's enough from you for now,' said the teacher. 'Anyone else?'

One of the boys put his hand up.

'Yes, Eric,' said the teacher.

'So how come you're not dead?' he asked Riley.

'Because I had a bulletproof vest on,' she replied.

'Sensible questions please, Eric,' said the teacher. Another boy put his hand up.

'Yes, Charlie,' said the teacher.

'How did you know about the assassination?' he asked.

'We overheard the gang in a cafe,' said Casey, 'and then developed a plan to be there to stop them.'

'Isn't that dangerous?' asked Ava.

'It is,' said Alex, 'but we had some help.'

'From who?' asked Ava.

'Unfortunately, the White House has classified that top secret so we can't say,' said Alex. There was a groan in the classroom.

'Sorry, guys,' said Casey, 'but this does bring us on to why we are here today.'

Riley stepped forward and asked the class to split into three groups.

'Each of us will be with one group,' she said. 'We will then be asking each group to come up with a dangerous situation you might face on the street and asking each group to come up with a way to handle that situation so no-one gets hurt.'

The teacher then took over to put them in groups and Riley, Casey and Alex each went to work with a group.

Riley's group was mainly girls, including Ava. They came up with a scenario where a girl was followed by a strange man.

'Okay, so what do you do in that situation?' asked Riley.

'Run away,' said one girl.

'Yeah, but what if he chases you and he's faster?' said another.

'I don't know,' said the first girl.

'Well, is there a way to avoid this situation?' asked Riley.

'Possibly not,' said Ava, 'but we could reduce the risk,' she added.

'How?' asked Riley.

'By never being out on our own, especially if it's late at night,' said Ava.

'Very good,' said Riley.

Casey's group was a mixture of boys and girls. They had very different ideas on how to deal with problems. The boys seemed to favour a physical response, whereas the girls wanted to think their way out of the situation. The group had come up with getting lost in a new city as their scenario. The group was divided over asking a stranger for directions.

'You mustn't talk to strangers,' said one of the boys.

'So how on earth can you find out where to go?' said one of the girls, sounding frustrated.

Casey stepped in, 'How about we think of safe strangers to ask?' she said.

'Like who?' asked one of the girls.

'Like a police officer,' said Charlie, who was in the group.

'Well done, Charlie,' said Casey, 'any others?'

The group came up with several more suggestions along the same lines.

Alex had ended up with most of the boys in the class. They seemed very focussed on a theme of drugs for their discussion. One of the boys was gloating that he'd tried taking pills at a party. Alex was pleased to see the reaction of the other boys was not to praise him or give him recognition for this, but rather to criticise him for his stupidity.

'Are you really that dumb, Oli?' said one of the lads.

'Now, boys,' said Alex, 'let's not be nasty. How about

you each tell us the best way to handle a situation where you're being offered drugs or pills.'

In turn each of the boys gave sensible suggestions such as saying no, even if your friends laughed at you. Alex was really pleased with the group discussion.

When the class came back together the teacher asked a child from each group to come to the front and share what their group had been discussing. That way the class could learn from the other groups they weren't in. All in all, the lesson was a huge success. The teacher asked the class to thank Riley, Casey and Alex.

They all shouted, 'Thank you!' and gave them a clap as they said their goodbyes and moved onto the next class.

In total they worked with three classes in the school, taking a break for lunch after the first two classes. At the end of the day, Agent Jacobs met them and took them back to their house in Lee Heights.

'I'll pick you up at the same time tomorrow,' he said. 'We've got a different school to do each day.'

'Thanks,' said Riley as they got out of the car.

'See you tomorrow,' said Casey.

As they entered the house, they went through to the kitchen to find Director Andrews sitting with Elsie drinking coffee.

'Good afternoon,' he said.

'Hi, sir,' said Riley. 'What are you doing here?'

'I'm here to let you know you'll be going home on Saturday,' he said.

None of them spoke. Instead they each sat down in the chairs around the table.

'Are you not pleased to be going home?' said Elsie.

'If we're honest, no,' said Riley. 'We've had such a great time here doing the training and then being able to work on Operation Legion. We will miss being here.'

'I appreciate that,' said Jack, 'which is why we've decided to involve you in regular operations. You'll have to wait for a new assignment but be assured your country will call on you again.'

'Thank you, sir,' said Riley, 'it's been an honour to serve.' The Director stood up from the table.

'I'll see you all on Saturday before your flights,' he said. 'Elsie, thank you for your help these last few months,' he added.

'Always a pleasure, Director,' she replied. With that, Jack left the house and headed back to DC.

'So,' said Elsie, 'I bet you three are all hungry.'

'We are,' said Alex.

'Okay, give me some space and I'll get dinner ready,' she said.

The three of them left her to it and went through to the lounge. Sitting down in the armchair, Casey said, 'I'm gonna miss being here.'

'We all are,' said Riley.

'But at least Jack has promised we will be back,' added Alex.

'True,' said Riley.

The rest of the week went past far too quickly. They visited lots of different schools and worked with hundreds of children. It was a great experience. They all found a new confidence through having conversations and leading small groups, something that would serve them well in the future. As Agent Jacobs picked them up from the last school on the Friday evening, there was a real sense it was all over. Everyone was very quiet in the car heading back to the house.

'Hey guys, cheer up. You'll be back here soon, I'm sure of it! Anyway, I'll be here in the morning to take you to the airport,' said Agent Jacobs.

Chapter 29

Going Home

Once they were ready for bed, they all said goodnight on the landing. Alex stayed put when Casey left for her room.

'Do you want to come in for a minute?' asked Riley.

'That'd be nice,' said Alex, 'it'll be our last chance for a while.'

She took his hand and led him into her room. As he'd done before he left the door open. She got onto the bed and he lay down next to her.

They stayed there looking into each other's eyes.

'I love you,' said Alex.

Riley's heart missed a beat. Had he really said those words? She put her hand on his cheek.

'l love you too,' she replied.

He learnt forward and kissed her. Their arms wrapped around each other and they lay there hugging for a while. Riley felt so safe in his arms. Ever since he'd saved her from falling into the helicopter wreckage, she'd loved being held by him.

Suddenly Riley yelped with pain.

'You okay?' asked Alex.

'It's the muscles in my back,' she replied, 'they're still a bit tender.'

'Do you want me to rub your back for you?' asked Alex.

'Would you mind?' she replied.

'No, not at all,' he said, sitting up. She moved into the middle of the bed and lay on her tummy. Alex sat next to her and gentle rubbed her back.

'Can you touch my skin?' she asked. He moved his hand up the back of her vest and gently slid his fingers over her skin.

'That tickles,' she said.

'Sorry,' he replied.

'No, I like it,' she said.

'Is the pain still there?' asked Alex.

'Just a little bit but this has helped,' she said.

After a while he slowed his hand down and took it out from under her top.

'We should get some sleep,' he said.

'Okay,' she said, 'and thank you for being so gentle.'

He just smiled, gave her a kiss and said, 'Good night,' before getting up to go to his own room.

Riley woke early on Saturday morning. As she sat up in bed a sadness filled her heart. She realised this was the last morning getting up in this room with her two best friends living in the house with her. The emotion soon switched from sadness to excitement as she thought about seeing her family again after several months of being away.

She pulled back the covers and got up out of bed. The bedroom floor was covered with clothes ready for packing. After her usual morning shower, she went to her wardrobe where one outfit remained on its hanger. She took out a pair of denim short dungarees and a white t-shirt and put them on. She decided to finish her packing after breakfast and made her way downstairs.

The others were in the kitchen munching on toast Elsie had put on the table moments before.

'Hi Riley,' said Casey spitting crumbs everywhere.

'Casey!' said Alex disapprovingly.

'Morning,' replied Riley.

'Take a seat, dear,' said Elsie, 'I've got the kettle on.'

Riley sat down next to Alex. He gave her a kiss on the cheek and said good morning. She smiled as she helped herself to toast. In her mind she didn't want this breakfast to end. For Riley this was perfect, sharing the start of each day with her two best friends, one of whom was also her boyfriend.

'How's your back?' asked Alex.

'Better, thanks,' said Riley.

'What was wrong with it?' asked Casey.

'Oh, the muscles were still hurting from last week,' said

Riley. 'What time is Agent Jacobs arriving?' Riley asked Elsie.

'About 10.00 a.m., dear, so you'll need to be packed by then.'

The others had already put their cases in the hall. Riley had noticed them on her way into the kitchen. She thought for a moment about the piles of clothes all over her floor. Her heart sank and the thought of packing them all away to leave.

'Are you looking forward to seeing Beth and Max?' asked Casey.

'Not really,' replied Riley, laughing. She paused and replied again. 'Honestly, yeah I am, I've missed them but that feeling will wear off about five minutes after I get home.'

'You never know,' said Alex, 'they may have calmed down in the last three months.'

'I doubt it,' replied Riley, 'it'd take more than a lightning bolt to sort those two out!'

The others started to laugh.

'Beth and Max are your sister and brother, aren't they?' said Elsie.

'Yes, they are,' said Riley, 'they're twins and very annoying.'

'What about you two, are you looking forward to seeing your parents Casey, and your dad, Alex?' asked Riley.

'I guess so,' said Casey.

'Yeah,' said Alex.

Alex sounded the most upbeat about going home. Perhaps it was something to do with the home he was going to. His dad treated him like an adult, he had no annoying siblings and the house was a nice place to live. Casey's place was the most run down of the three and her dad worked so hard just to make ends meet. Riley's was in between the two but was occupied by the twins! All in all, they were definitely happiest where they were.

'Right, you lot,' said Elsie as breakfast finished, 'get yourselves ready to go.' They all got up from the table.

'Riley, do you want a hand with packing?' asked Casey.

'Yes, please,' she said, thinking again of the mess of clothes on her floor.

Alex stayed to help Elsie clear away and the girls went upstairs to finish Riley's packing.

'Jeez,' said Casey as they walked into Riley's room.

'Yeah, I know it's a mess!' replied Riley.

'Come on then,' said Casey, 'let's get started.'

The two of them knelt down on the floor and started to place clothes in the case.

'Have you checked your drawers?' asked Casey.

'I think so,' said Riley.

'Do it again,' said Casey, 'just in case you've missed something.'

'Okay,' said Riley, getting up from the floor.

Riley went to the drawers and opened each one in turn. They were all empty. She then went to her bedside table and pulled open the little drawer on the front of it. Lying inside was her sketchbook and some pencils.

'Oops,' she said as she lifted them out to show Casey.

'See!' said Casey. 'How upset would you be if you'd left them behind?'

'Very,' replied Riley as she knelt back down to place the sketchbook in the case.

It didn't take the girls long to pack everything. Casey had to sit on the case to squash it shut while Riley fumbled around under her trying to get the zip around. Finally, it was done and between them they started to lug the case down the stairs. Alex heard the commotion from the lounge, where he was now sitting. He jumped up, ran up the stairs to meet the girls half way.

'I've got it from here,' he said, lifting the case with ease and taking it to the hall.

'Thanks,' said Riley.

As the girls reached the bottom of the stairs, the doorbell rang. Riley walked forward and opened the door. On the front step were Agent Jacobs and Director Andrews.

'Morning, Riley,' said the Director.

'You guys ready to go?' asked Agent Jacobs. Casey and Alex appeared in the doorway.

'Yes, we're ready,' said Alex. They took their bags to the large 4x4 and loaded them in. Then returned to the front door step. Elsie was now standing there ready to see them off.

'Well,' she said, 'this is goodbye for now.'

Riley went over to her and gave her a hug. The others followed suit and they all said their goodbyes.

Director Andrews said, 'It's goodbye for me too, I'm staying here with Elsie until Agent Jacobs returns from the airport.'

They didn't hug the Director as that didn't feel appropriate. However, there was plenty of hand shaking being exchanged.

'I'll see you all soon,' said the Director.

'I hope so, sir,' said Riley.

'You will,' he replied. 'I meant it when I said you are one of the Service's top teams!' he added.

'Thanks sir,' they all replied.

'Right, let's get going,' said Agent Jacobs, 'you have a flight to catch.'

They all got into the 4x4 and waved to Elsie as the car pulled off of the driveway.

'I'll miss those three,' she said as she and the Director went inside the house.

'Oh, they'll be back,' he said, 'and sooner than you think.'

The 4x4 made its way through the streets of Arlington towards the Potomac River and the Ronald Reagan National Airport. It didn't take them all that long and before they knew it, they were standing at the drop off zone saying goodbye to Agent Jacobs.

'Thanks for everything,' said Casey.

'My pleasure,' said Agent Jacobs. 'It's just a shame Riley couldn't be here to say goodbye,' he added.

'Hey, I'm right here and I'm not invisible!' she exclaimed.

'I know, I'm only messing,' replied Agent Jacobs. 'Stay safe, you three, and I'll see you soon.'

'Will do,' said Alex, shaking his hand.

They stood and watched as their last connection with the world of the Secret Service drove away.

As they walked into the airport to find the check-in desk, they really were just three regular teenagers travelling home to their families. Once they'd got rid of the heavy bags at check-in, they made their way through security to the departure lounge and found a coffee shop.

'What do you want to drink?' asked Riley.

'Coffee, please,' replied Alex and Casey. They sat down while Riley ordered at the counter before joining them.

'What time is the flight?' asked Casey, realising after she'd asked that she was holding a boarding pass with it written on.

'12.35 p.m.,' replied Alex. 'We will be home by 4.00 p.m.'

'Here you go,' said Riley, handing her friends their drinks.

'Thanks,' said Casey.

'So, landing at 4.00 p.m. then,' said Riley.

'Yeah,' said Alex, 'is your mom coming to meet you?'

'Yes,' said Riley.

'I think we are all being met at the airport,' said Casey.

'I guess that's where this adventure will end,' said Alex.

Riley put her arm round him and picked up her coffee mug.

'Here's to more adventures then,' she said.

The others picked up their mugs and replied, 'More adventures!'

A call for their flight came over the tannoy. They finished their drinks and headed for the departure gate. At the gate they showed the steward their boarding cards.

'Okay you're all together in row 19, on the left-hand side,' she said.

'Thank you,' said Alex as they picked up their hand luggage and walked down the ramp to the plane.

They took their seats, Alex by the window, then Riley with Casey in the aisle seat. They all watched out of the small window as they took off, and the sights of Washington soon disappeared from view. Fortunately, before they could start yet another conversation about how they'd miss life in DC the steward came by offering food and drinks.

As the flight went on, their conversation soon moved to planning their next meet up.

'Well, we only have one week in school before the summer!' said Casey.

'Then it'll be my birthday,' said Riley.

'Yeah of course, we will have to do something together for that,' said Casey.

'Let's give our families a couple of days with us before we ask them for time together,' said Alex.

'Okay,' said Riley, 'but just a couple. I don't think I could stand being away from you guys longer than that!'

Time seemed to go quickly on the plane. You might even say it flew by!

'Seat belts on please, ladies and gentlemen. We are coming into land at Jackson State Airport,' said the stewardess.

Once they'd disembarked and collected their baggage, they made their way through to where their families were waiting.

'Riley, Riley!' shouted the twins the moment they saw her.

They didn't wait for her to clear the barrier. Pulling away from their mum they rushed under the railing over to their big sister.

'See what I mean?' said Riley to Casey and Alex. 'Delightful for five minutes!' The others smiled and headed towards their parents.

'Hi, Mom,' said Riley, giving her mum a huge hug.

'Hello, my lovely girl. How are you?' replied her mum.

'Doing great,' said Riley. Casey hugged her mum and dad who'd both come to meet her. Alex did the same with his father.

'You ready to go, son?' asked Mr Manning.

'Yeah, just give me a moment,' replied Alex. He turned to the girls. 'We're going,' he said.

Riley and Casey stopped what they were doing with their families and turned to Alex. This was it! This was the moment they went their separate ways! Riley's eyes began to swell with tears.

'Come here,' said Alex, hugging both girls. 'I'll see you in a couple of days,' he said.

'FaceTime later,' said Casey stepping back to give them a moment. Alex wiped away Riley's tears.

'Hey, come on, it's not over and I'll see you very soon,' he said.

'I love you,' she replied.

'I love you too,' he said hugging her again.

After they'd said their goodbyes all three families went their separate ways. Riley was quiet in the car, although you wouldn't have been able to tell as the twins bombarded her with questions about her time in Washington.

'Guys, guys, let Riley breathe, please,' said their mum. 'There's plenty of time to ask her questions,' she added, 'like how long you and Alex have been an item!'

'Mom!' said Riley. 'Is it that obvious?'

'Oh yes!' said her mother, smiling at her. Riley smiled back.

'Not long,' she said, 'since the fourth of July actually.'

'Ah,' said her mum, 'that's one way to celebrate Independence Day!'

'Mom!' said Riley in a raised pitch.

Her mum laughed, 'I'm only joking, darling, I'm really happy for you. He's a lovely guy.'

'Thanks, Mom,' said Riley.

Chapter 30

The Birthday

Soon after they were pulling onto the driveway and home! Mrs Bennett helped Riley with her bags. Beth took her mum's keys and opened the door to let them all in. There was a welcome home banner hanging in the hall waiting for Riley.

'The twins made it,' said Mrs Bennett.

'Thanks guys, it's cool,' said Riley. Beth and Max smiled before running off to the lounge together to put the television on.

'Well that didn't last long,' said Riley.

'I'm amazed they stayed around as long as they did,' replied her mum. Riley gave her mum another hug.

'It's so good to see you,' she said. Her mum smiled.

'It's great to see you too. We've missed you these last three months.'

They went through to the kitchen and Riley sat at the island while her mum put the kettle on.

'So, tell me all about the last three months then,' said her mum.

Riley's mind quickly ran through all they'd seen and done. She thought about the terrorist cells they'd stopped and the people they'd met and worked with. She thought about NASA anti-gravity suits, aircraft carriers, guns, bombs and helicopters.

'Where do I start?' she said.

'At the beginning,' replied her mum. 'Where were you living?'

'Well, we had a lovely house in Lee Heights in Arlington. We each had our own room and we had a housekeeper called Elsie who looked after us,' said Riley.

'That sounds good. I wish we had a housekeeper!' replied her mum.

'We do, don't we?' said Riley raising her eyebrows at her mum.

'Hey, cheeky!' said her mum smiling.

'So, tell me what you've been doing all this time,' said her mum.

'Well, we met the President again,' said Riley, 'in fact one night we had dinner with him in the residence of the White House.'

'Wow,' said her mum, 'you are an incredibly lucky girl.'

'I know, Mom,' replied Riley.

'So, what else?' asked her mum.

'Well for the first few weeks they gave us some training for our work in schools. It was quite tough as we had to fit our own school work around it,' said Riley.

'Oh, that reminds me. Mr Willis contacted me asking where your last assignment was,' said her mum.

'I've got it in my bag. It's done,' replied Riley.

'Good,' said her mum. 'I'm proud of you doing this and keeping up with your studies too!'

Mrs Bennett poured some coffee into mugs and sat down at the island with Riley.

'Tell me about being an Ambassador,' said her mum.

Riley went on to tell her about the lessons they'd done and the schools they'd been in. She told her mum about the group conversations they'd led and some of the interesting questions they'd been asked. After they'd drunk their coffees Riley took her bags upstairs to her room to unpack. As she opened the door, she saw her old room with the bed and rug and her table with the computer sat on it. She dropped her bags and went over to the bed. Diving face first she sank into the pillow. She breathed in. That familiar smell of home was still there. After a moment she turned over and lay there. Her thoughts quickly turned to Alex and Casey. She wondered how they were getting on.

Casey and her parents had arrived home around the same time as Riley did.

'I'll get that, Dad,' said Casey, lifting the bag from the

back of the car. Mr Johnson looked at his wife and raised his eyebrows, probably wondering who this self-sufficient, polite teenager was! The three of them went inside. Casey put her bags upstairs to sort out and then came down to spend some time with her parents.

'Do either of you want a coffee?' she asked, putting the kettle on. Slightly taken aback that Casey was offering, they both hesitated before saying yes.

'You've changed, young lady,' said her mum.

'No, I haven't,' replied Casey.

'Yeah, you have,' said her dad, 'and it's wonderful to see.'

'So, tell us all about Washington,' said her mum, 'we've missed you and want to hear all about it.'

Casey also thought of all the things she couldn't say before telling them about the house and the schools they'd worked in. She told them about their days off exploring DC. including the day they pretended to be tourists.

'Sounds like an amazing experience,' said her dad.

If only you knew! Casey thought to herself!

Alex and his father didn't go straight home. Instead they headed for their favourite restaurant and had something to eat. Mr Manning wasn't one for cooking if he could help it. He also asked Alex about his adventures. Alex decided to take the opportunity to tell his father about him and Riley.

'Son, I'm thrilled, she's a wonderful girl,' said his father.

'Thanks, Dad, we've got something really special,' said Alex.

'There's something special between the three of you that goes way beyond a lightning bolt,' replied his father.

'Yeah, there most certainly is,' said Alex.

After dinner they made their way back to the house. Alex took his bags upstairs and sorted out his clothes. He sat at his desk and turned on the computer. He connected to FaceTime and waited to see if the others appeared. It didn't take long for both girls to appear on his screen. He almost sighed with relief as if his life depended on the call.

'You okay?' asked Riley.

'Yeah, just missing you both,' said Alex.

'It's only been three hours!' said Casey.

'Yeah, I know,' said Alex, 'I'll be a wreck in three days!' The girls laughed, but both appreciated being missed by him.

They spent some time chatting about their arrival home.

'My parents think I've changed,' said Casey.

'Changed how?' said Riley.

'No idea,' said Casey, 'but I think it's a good change.'

'Well my mom had figured out about me and Alex by the time the car left the airport!' said Riley.

'Really!' said Alex. 'What did you say?'

'Nothing,' said Riley, 'she just knew. Good thing is she's happy about it.'

'So's my dad,' said Alex, 'I told him over dinner this evening. Apparently, you're a wonderful girl,' he added.

'Well, yes I am,' said Riley, laughing.

'I'm glad your parents are all okay with this,' said Casey.

'We're glad you are,' said Riley. 'You two mean the world to me,' she added.

'Don't go sloppy on me now!' said Casey, laughing. They talked for a while longer and agreed to speak again on Sunday evening.

'Let's meet up for coffee after school on Monday,' said Riley.

'At our old coffee shop by the library,' said Casey.

'Great idea,' said Alex, 'I've missed that place.'

They said their goodbyes and went back to spending some catch up time with their families.

Riley helped her mum get dinner ready.

'Home-made spaghetti! I've missed this,' she said.

'We need to talk,' said her mum.

'What about?' said Riley, sounding a little apprehensive.

'Your birthday!' said her mum. Riley smiled.

'What about it?' she asked.

'Well it's your sixteenth so do you want to do anything special, like a party?'

THE BIRTHDAY

Riley was thinking that all the people in her life worked for the FBI, CIA and Secret Service. A big party was probably not the way to go.

'To be honest, I'd be happy if Alex, Casey and their families came over and joined us for the evening,' she said.

'Okay,' said her mum, 'that sounds like a nice idea.'

The rest of the weekend went quickly. All three of them spent time with family, but couldn't help thinking about their experiences in Washington and London. Being able to talk together was crucial as there was a great deal they couldn't share with their families.

Monday morning came all too soon. Riley took the bus to school and was amazed to find no-one making a comment about her for the entire journey. She was slightly disappointed as she had a few moves Koba had taught her ready to try if they did! Well in her mind she had. The reality was Riley had learnt to always use her powers and abilities for the good of others, even if their intentions weren't so honourable.

Casey met her at the entrance to school.

'Feels weird being back here, doesn't it?' said Casey.

'Yeah, it does,' said Riley. 'Can you remember where our lockers are?'

'You know, I've been in that many schools recently, it may take a while,' said Casey laughing.

Mr Willis was pleased to see them both again and Riley made a point of handing him her completed assignment.

After school they made their way to the cafe by the library. As they walked in, they saw Alex sat on their sofa at the back of the cafe. He'd already brought them both milkshakes.

'Aw, that's sweet of you,' said Riley, giving him a kiss.

'How have you both been?' asked Alex.

'Okay,' said Casey.

'Missing DC,' said Riley.

'Yeah, I think that's true for us all,' said Alex.

They sat and talked about their day and the memories of their time in Arlington.

'Oh, my mom wants you and your parents over to ours on August 1st,' said Riley.

'For your birthday?' asked Alex.

'Yeah,' said Riley, 'there's no-one else I'd rather spend it with.'

'Sounds great,' said Casey, 'have you thought what you'd like?'

'Probably some new clothes,' said Riley.

'Now there's a surprise,' said Alex. 'You two can get them without me this time,' he added, having a flashback to the time they all went to the shopping mall.

The next couple of weeks saw the end of the school year and the summer break begin. The weather got steadily hotter which, for Riley, always meant her birthday was near. Finally, the day came. August 1st was a Friday, but a Friday with no school. Riley woke early, mainly because the twins came bursting into her room at about 7.00 a.m. with presents and cards. Her mother followed soon after with a cup of coffee, which was far more welcome at that hour on a non-school day.

Riley sat on her bed with her family as she unwrapped her presents. The twins had got her new pyjamas and her mum had bought her a beautiful silk dress.

'I thought you might like to wear it out to dinner with that handsome boyfriend of yours,' said Mrs Bennett.

Riley blushed. 'Thanks, Mom,' she said.

They spent the morning getting ready for their guests. Casey and Alex arrived early afternoon, several hours before their parents. This gave Riley some time with her friends. The three of them went to the local park and had ice cream. They sat in the warm summer sun making plans for the summer together.

'Are either of you going away?' asked Casey. Her family could never afford a holiday so summers were always spent at home.

'I'm not sure,' said Riley. 'Mom's not mentioned anything.'

'My dad wants us to go and stay in this huge apartment

in Florida,' said Alex. 'It belongs to one of his business partners who is travelling around Europe this summer. It's big enough for all of us!'

Riley paused for a moment, her brain running through an idea. 'Well, why don't we all go then!' she said.

'What about our parents and the twins?' said Casey.

'The place would fit us all,' said Alex.

'There we go!' said Riley. 'Can you ask your dad what he thinks to the idea?'

'Yeah,' said Alex, 'I'll ask him tonight at your party.'

Meanwhile in Florida, Air Force Commander Adams was about to leave her office at the Kennedy Space Centre for the evening when a junior officer came in.

'Ma'am, there's a call for you from the UK Observatory at Jodrell Bank.'

Riley, Alex and Casey made their way back to Riley's house to find all the parents in the garden having drinks. Riley's mum had set up the barbecue as the weather was so good. Mr Johnson was busy cooking sausages on it.

'That's surreal,' said Casey, 'my dad cooking in your garden!'

'Happy birthday,' said Alex's father, handing Riley a small present. They gathered round as she unwrapped it. It was a small blue box. She lifted the lid so see a thin silver chain with a pendant on. The pendant was in the shape of a lightning bolt.

'Wow,' said Riley, 'it's beautiful. Thank you, Mr Manning.'

'Oh, don't thank me,' he said. 'Alex chose it, I just helped pay for it.' Riley turned to Alex.

'Thank you,' she said, 'it's a beautiful gift.' She kissed him.

'Perfect for a beautiful girl then,' he replied. Riley turned bright red, before giving him a big hug.

Just like Casey, her father was good at killing mushy moments and chose that moment to say, 'Sausages, anyone?'

The distraction was perfectly timed and everyone wandered over to the barbecue to get some food. Alex pulled his father to one side and mentioned the idea of everyone going to Florida. He was delighted when his father said it was an excellent idea. Mr Manning wasted no time in offering the holiday to the entire group. After some discussion on dates and calls to work, they all agreed to go.

'This has to be the best birthday ever!' said Riley.

Back in Washington, there was a knock on the door.

'Come in,' said the President.

An aide walked in, 'Sir, Air Force Commander Adams is on line one for you from NASA. You need to take this.'

The President picked up the phone on his desk and pressed the button for line one.

'Jenny, this is the President. What can I do for you?'

'Good afternoon, sir,' she replied. 'Sorry to bother you, Mr President, but we have a very serious problem!'

About the Author

Hi, I'm Andy and this is my second Riley Bennett book. I hope you've already enjoyed reading my first book (*The Courage Within*). Here is a little bit about me. I was born in London, but I've lived in the north-west of England since 1994. I'm a dad to Grace and Sam. Both Grace and I have had epilepsy, something we share in common with Riley.

I'm a self-taught artist, which can be a challenge as I have a visual impairment. However, I love being creative, which is why I've enjoyed writing this book for you. I hope you've enjoyed reading it. Keep an eye out for the next Riley Bennett book, called *The Stellar Alliance*.

Other Books by this Author

The Courage Within
(The Riley Bennett Series)

The Adventures of Ben the Mouse
Book One

The Adventures of Ben the Mouse
Book Two

Lightning Source UK Ltd.
Milton Keynes UK
UKHW010712150720
366581UK00001B/256